RAINBOW'S END

Rainbow's End

Edwina Orth

RAINBOW'S END

iUniverse books may be ordered through booksellers or by contacting:

iUniverse
1663 Liberty Drive
Bloomington, IN 47403
www.iuniverse.com
1-800-Authors (1-800-288-4677)

ISBN: 978-1-4917-6045-1 (sc)
ISBN: 978-1-4917-6044-4 (e)

Library of Congress Control Number: 2015902251

Print information available on the last page.

iUniverse rev. date: 02/09/2014

PROLOGUE

A large dark-brown-and-tan dog loped across the snowy field. He knew he had a mission, but it was not clear yet. He stopped and sat with ears cocked. Then he heard it again, a soft whimpering, as if someone was in trouble.

He turned his head and caught it again. It was close by now. He'd wait and listen. Duke's sensitive ears and instincts made him in tune with whatever it was that was causing him to tremble.

In the distance, he saw a figure stumbling toward him. The figure was on the ground, trying to get up. He raced to her side and licked her face. She cried in fear as she saw the white teeth in the large head. He sat and just looked at her with eyes that were sending out warm messages. He licked her face again, and she put her arms around his head and buried her face in his fur.

He watched her get up, and he began to walk toward some summer cottages nearby. She followed him, shuffling one foot before another. He led her to a cottage made of wood and stone, with a cellar door without a lock. Soon they were inside, and the girl sat down to catch her breath.

He looked at her and saw weak tears running down her face. Yes, this was it. He would stay with her. He would guard her and help her. This must be his mission, what he was meant to do.

CHAPTER ONE

Jason stopped to rest, heaving and shaking with the cold. He looked at his watch and saw that he had been hurrying to put lots of space between him and his uncle for several hours. It had begun to snow about an hour ago, and the wind was sharp and biting. He grabbed a birch tree trunk for support. He gritted his teeth as he almost fell. He knew he had to keep going until he found shelter.

After a few moments, he started walking again. His head was aching, and his throat stung with the cold air. He plodded along for a few more yards, and then he noticed he was near a lake. There were several summer cottages close by, and Jason hoped there was one he could get into. Breaking and entering was not his forte, but he was desperate.

The first cottage was boarded up as tight as Fort Knox, and he knew he did not have the strength to force an entry. A little further on was a wood-and-stone odd-shaped cottage that had a sloping cellar door. It too had boarded windows, and the front door was enclosed with a metal grid. He tried to lift the cellar door but found it padlocked. Jason dug under the snow until he found a rock heavy enough to use. With several hard blows, he cracked open the lock. It took all his strength to lift up the door. He saw a few steps leading to a heavy wooden door. He pressed the old-fashioned latch, and the door was opened into a dark, cold room.

He rummaged in his knapsack and found his flashlight. He looked around and saw that the room was used for storage, and there were beach chairs, fishing gear, a canoe, and paddles. He saw steps leading to the first floor and what looked like a switch at the top for a light. He tried the switch, but no light came on. *I need to find the circuit-breaker box, if there is one*, he thought.

He pushed open the door at the top of the stairs and found he was in the kitchen. The circuit breaker was on the wall near the door leading to the porch outside, and when he pushed the switch, he heard a slight noise. When he tried the light switch, the room was flooded with light. Thank God they had not turned the electricity off for the winter. He sank into a kitchen chair and rested his head on his arms. God, he was exhausted. He had been out in the cold, walking and sometimes running, for hours.

Finally, he decided to look for heat. He hoped it was electric and not propane. He found the thermostat and clicked it on. With a sigh of relief, he set it for seventy degrees. He wandered into the living room, and when he saw the large sofa, he nearly ran to it. He removed his shoes and wet socks, his layers of flannel shirts, and his sweater. He found a blue-and-white woolen blanket on a chair, and he was soon wrapped in warmth. He gently fell into a deep, restful sleep— the first he'd had in several weeks.

He slowly opened his eyes, and for a moment, he did not remember where he was. He looked at his watch and saw it was six thirty. *It must be morning*, he thought as he had entered the house about five o'clock.

He used the bathroom, but he did not have water yet. *I hope I can get the water on soon.* He looked around for any clothes he could wear and found a pair of jeans and a man's flannel shirt that almost fit. In the closet, he also found a pair of bedroom slippers that were about one size too large. He put them on, grateful for small miracles. He put his wet clothes on hangers in the bathroom to dry.

He thought it might be okay to turn on the water and hoped it was warm enough. He thought again and decided to wait awhile to make sure it was warm enough for that. Looking through the cupboards, he found powdered milk and oatmeal. Both were in glass jars, so the mice had not found them.

He took a large pan and went outside to gather snow. He melted some on the electric stove and then let it boil for a few minutes. Afterward, he mixed the powdered milk, oatmeal, and water. The oatmeal and tea were soon on the table, and he dug in, his hunger overwhelming. He wrote down the cost of the food as best he could figure it and hoped he could someday repay the owners.

After eating, he turned on the main water knob. He heard it fill the hot-water heater and breathed a sigh of pleasure. A hot bath! What luxury!

When the water was warm enough, he did the dishes and then washed as best he could. The water was not hot enough for a shower or bath, but it felt good to be clean again. He sat in the kitchen and read some old magazines. He tried to figure out where to turn or what to do. He had no warm clothes and no food or any way to buy some. He gave a frustrated sigh. *I still feel exhausted. Perhaps I can sleep again. There's nothing else to do, and I can't seem to have any ideas.* Wrapped in the blanket, he soon was asleep.

Jason awoke with a feeling of cold—cold air. Groggily, he opened his eyes and looked around. He could feel a presence in the room. As his eyes became adjusted to the dim light, he saw an outline of a person—what the hell—and a dog?

"Well, you finally surfaced. Who are you? What are you doing here in this empty house?"

The dog moved as if to get closer to Jason, but a sharp command "sit" and a tug on his lead made him stop.

"Well, am I going to call 911, or are you going to explain?" Again, the woman said "sit," as the dog tried to creep closer to Jason. The dog, paying no attention, inched closer. Jason could see large brown eyes, lots of sharp-looking teeth, and a very large brown noble-looking head. *What breed of dog was he? Was he a Doberman pinscher or perhaps a German shepherd?*

The dog moved closer and began to lick Jason's hand. "Sit," she said again, only softer this time. She sounded puzzled.

"You must not be a robber or worse, or Duke would have growled long ago."

"Please, whoever you are, give me a chance to explain."

"Okay, go ahead. Convince me not to call 911."

After a moment of thinking how to best tell her, he began. "My dad's name was Richard. We were very close, and he always supported me as I planned my college courses. He died six months ago, leaving all his estate to me. However, the money would be held in trust until I was twenty-one years old.

My father made the will quite a few years earlier and had not updated it since. He put the estate in the hands of his brother Tomas, as he thought his brother would guide me if he were not here. My uncle was never close to me, but he idolized my brother Gary. Gary was quiet natured and not a gifted scholar. He had features similar to our uncle Tomas and was two years older than I. Gary died in a boating accident a year ago. Since then, my uncle hasn't been even civil to me. This is especially difficult as my uncle moved into the house after my dad died, and he knew he was now in charge.

"My uncle is a tall, imposing-looking man with dark blue eyes that are hooded and shrewd. He has a limp that is hardly noticeable from a skiing accident as a teen. He was not at all like my father.

"My uncle slowly became cold and distant and more critical of all I did or planned. I was twenty years old and had just finished my second year at college when my dad died. I talked to Dad about changing colleges and taking courses in oceanography. I had been studying business, as I thought that was what my dad had expected of me. But no, he had been supportive and agreed that I could apply to an oceanography school the next semester.

"I found a job for the summer months—at a department store as a bookkeeper. I enjoyed the work. It was a way to earn money for my next semester. I was ready to return to college, if my uncle was ready to pay the tuition out of my inheritance.

"I sent a letter and application to Washington State School of Oceanography in Seattle, Washington, but had not received any notice about my acceptance. My uncle had not broached the subject of the new school, and when I reminded him, he'd said, 'I'll have to think it through more carefully before giving money away. The courses you want to take aren't worth much on the market. Perhaps you should just get a job and learn what it is to work for a change.'

"Anger raged through me. I managed to keep civil as I replied, 'Well, my dad always agreed that I could take courses in oceanography. I believe there are always openings in scientific research and teaching, even if the field is not as open as others.' My uncle turned away with a grunt of disgust.

"A few weeks later, I noticed that some paintings had been removed from the wall in the living room. These were my dad's favorite ones, and when I questioned their removal, my uncle said they were going to be cleaned professionally. My dad's collection of expensive Lalique was also missing. When I asked my uncle, Tomas, he just shrugged. He did not answer and just walked away.

"My uncle skillfully kept me waiting for months, and October gave way to November. I knew it was too late for this semester. I thought my uncle should be helping me, not putting roadblocks in my way.

"I realized that something was very wrong. The time had passed for me to go back to college and begin my new studies. I hadn't heard from the college yet, and that was a puzzle. Even if they were unable to accept me, they would have sent a reply to my request.

"My uncle did not give me any reason for the delay, and when I asked, I was told that nothing had been decided yet.

"Who could I turn to? Who could help me in this battle against my uncle? I have no money for a lawyer, as my uncle Tomas has control of everything until I'm twenty-one. Well, I thought I can ask my father's attorney if he will help me. It can't hurt, and time is going by when I should be at college, not wasting my time here in a place that doesn't feel like home anymore.

"I called my father's attorney, Mr. Ralph Shumen, and explained my problem. Mr. Shumen said he was so booked up that it would take two months before I could see him. I knew he was stalling. Come to think of it, he was also a friend of my uncle Tomas. In my gut, I knew I was out on a limb with nowhere to turn.

"Earlier in the week, I saw my uncle and Mr. Shumen walking together. They were deep in conversation and did not see me hiding behind some trees. When I saw a car coming toward the driveway, I hid behind a garden shed and watched. A policeman waved to my uncle, and the three men stood and talked for a long while. Finally, the policeman nodded his head and soon drove away. My uncle and the attorney went into the house, still talking and agreeing on something."

Jason stopped for breath. He looked at the woman, and she shrugged. "Take a breather. I am not going anywhere."

Jason began again. "I was scared. I had no doubt at all that my uncle was not the person my father had known and trusted. He had become greedy and mean. I was certain that the attorney and my uncle were plotting something evil. I slipped into the house. I left my jacket and boots in the kitchen and crept upstairs. I could hear the two men talking, as I was just above them and their words were clear.

"'Well, everything's all set, Ralph. Tonight after dinner, the police will pick Jason up and take him to jail. He is going to be charged with stealing two expensive paintings and several expensive Lalique figurines. Each of them is worth over $2,000. I will claim that he took them to the store in town, and of course, there will be proof that he brought them

7

in and received money in an envelope for each item. He is on the security surveillance tape, and my man will also swear that he got the money. It's a perfect setup. Soon, Jason will be out of the way, and the whole estate and all it is worth will be mine. Of course, you will get your share just like we agreed, Ralph.'"

"I knew I had to move fast. I had to get away. But where could I go? Well, I would decide that later when I was away from this house. That's if I could get away without being caught.

"I packed a few things in a backpack. I put in a flashlight, a folding knife, and matches. I silently crept down the stairs and out the back door. I had to leave my boots and winter jacket, as they were too close to the room the men were in.

"When I was out of sight of the house, I ran into the woods. I knew it was a longer way to the lake, but I needed to keep out of sight. I hoped to find a summer cottage where I could seek shelter until I figured out what to do.

"It seemed like hours and hours of walking, running, and then resting for a few moments. It got colder, and the wind picked up. There was a smell of snow in the air. I was so cold I knew I wouldn't last much longer. My breath was razor sharp, and my eyes could barely see ahead.

"I was about to give up when I saw the lake and some buildings. I had come through the cold and snow and found refuge. Soon I was able to get inside. I almost fell into a chair.

"I sat and said something almost like a prayer. 'I am so glad to be here in this summer house. I am warm and alive. I'll put my troubles aside for now and be grateful for this miracle.'"

Without thinking, Jason had been stroking the dog's head and shoulders. If a dog could purr, this one purred. The dog kept his eyes on Jason, and they were warm and loving. The woman tried to pull him away, but he planted his front feet and balked. He seemed to have bonded with this stranger.

She had listened quietly until he finished. Then the questions began. "Do you believe the local police are working with your uncle? That's really hard to believe."

"Well, not all of them; just this Ralph and my uncle's lawyer. That is one thing I'm sure of. My uncle is a respected businessman and looked up to by many. People would take his word against mine every time. I am twenty years old, and I'm not in my uncle's league at all. My word would never be accepted. I don't know where to turn or whom to turn to."

She sat very still for a few minutes, and he let her have her moment for thought. She asked a good question and did not seem to be angry or suspicious anymore.

She sat and looked at him for a few minutes. When she smiled, a sudden zing went up and down his spine. Wow— what? By God, she was beautiful. Her smile transformed her into an elfin-like pixie. She had a mischievous look on her face.

Then she said, "My name is Lyndell, and I have a confession to make. I too am living in an empty summer cottage. It is a few houses down toward town. I came here to get away from a mean drunk of a man three weeks ago. I got a job here as a waitress at the Corner Deli and hope to get enough money to leave this place in a few weeks. I want to put more miles between here and there as soon as possible. I saw you from a distance yesterday, and I had to make certain you were not someone looking for me.

"You need help, as you have no warm clothes that I can see, and food is a few miles away. Why don't I go to work and bring something to eat? I can get food half priced where I work—my boss asks no questions—I can cook if I have to on your stove. Is that an okay idea?"

Jason had a million questions but kept still and decided to wait. She might not come back. She might bring the police or, worse, his uncle. He had to trust someone, he thought. He didn't have many options right now. For some reason, he trusted her. He had to trust someone, didn't he?

The woman moved into the light, and he could see her clearly now. Her hair was light brown, held back with a clip of some kind. Her eyes were blue gray. She looked about sixteen and tired. He couldn't tell much about her form, as she had on bulky clothes for warmth. Then she smiled, and the dimple in her cheek almost made him gasp. It transformed her. She looked like an Irish elf, full of secrets. "I'll be here about four o'clock with food. By the way, you don't have much food here, do you?"

Jason laughed. "No, just some crackers and a half box of cookies that the mice have left for me. So I'll appreciate anything you can bring."

"Okay. I'll see you later then. I have to eat and be back at my place before it gets dark. I begin early in the morning. I have the six-to-two-o'clock shift. I won't be late. Duke will be with me, as he watches my back all the time." She pulled the lead, and Duke went with her to the door. She looked back over her shoulder, and she had to say, "Come, Duke," before he moved again. "If you can, it will be good if you can have some water hot for tea. See you about four."

After she had gone, Jason sat and recalled her visit. Who was she? Was her story true or just a cover-up for something? She might even be a policewoman with that guard dog of hers. Maybe he was nuts to trust her. *Well, what's done is done,* he thought. *Tonight will tell, and I have no place to go or anyone else to trust anyway.*

CHAPTER TWO

True to her word, Lyndell came to his cellar door about three thirty. Jason looked lovingly at the frozen precooked fish, as well as the salad, lima beans, and French bread. She brought butter and a large slice of cake. "Oh lord, a bit of heaven, that's what this is. Thanks, Lyndell."

She fed Duke first and led him outside to have some freedom. She watched as he raced around the area, never going far from her by the cellar door. When he came back inside, he sat by Jason's feet, content to be close to him.

The sky was dark when they finished their meal. "Thanks, Lyndell, for the food and its preparation. I was starved." He gave her a lopsided smile. She nodded as if to say *You're welcome.*

Lyndell put the leftover scraps of food in a paper bag. She would take them to the recycle bin tomorrow. She sat and looked at Jason, making him feel old—well, not old but odd. *What is she thinking?*

Lyndell was thinking that he was a very handsome young man. She did not know many men. Her growing years had been lonely, and she did not have many contacts with her age group. Jason had dark brown hair and hazel eyes that were clear and honest looking. He was not too tall, about five foot nine. He also looked like he kept in good condition, as he had survived a long hike here. Could he be someone she could trust? For some reason, she trusted him anyway.

She stopped gawking and said, "Sorry, I was off somewhere." She began to explain what had been going on in her mind all afternoon. "Just listen, Jason, and don't say a word until I am finished, okay?"

He nodded and sat up straighter. Duke walked around the room and then settled by Lyndell. He seemed to be content to be a two-person dog. Lyndell patted his head, and the dog moved closer to her.

Jason looked at Lyndell and noted her serious face and steady gaze.

"Jason, you have to leave here right away. If I found this house occupied, he will too. He has the police to help him, and if he finds you here, you will have no way to defend yourself. I have some money saved for my bus ride west. I have no special destination; I just need to put more space between him and me. We can get you some warm clothes at Walmart tomorrow, get on the bus, and be off by nine o'clock. When we run out of money, I can get a job as a waitress at a bus depot or large truck service area. They are always looking for relief waitresses. There may be odd jobs you can find as well. Give it a moment of thought, but I have a feeling that your uncle is not far away right now."

Jason eyed her nervously. How could he not do all she recommended? She was offering him a way to put miles between him and his uncle. Also, there was her offer of clean warm clothes. If they rode west, Seattle would be his goal. "Do you think I should leave here tonight?"

"Yes, I do. Come and sleep at my place. It is well hidden, and no one can tell if there is anyone living there, at least from the outside."

"Lyndell, I can't let you do this for me. I don't want you to use your savings for my clothes or bus fare. Also, if we get caught, you will be in trouble—big time."

"I can't just leave you here to be put in jail to satisfy your uncle's greed. It is my money, and I know you will repay me when you get a job."

Jason sat and pondered her plan. He finally gave her his hand and said, "Thanks, Lyndell. I don't know why you want to do this for me, a stranger, but I will do whatever I can to repay you as soon as possible."

"Thank you, Jason." She looked at him again and hoped she had not made a mistake in trusting him. She noted his face, with a small scar under his right eye, and his steady gaze. *He's not at all like my stepfather or Gabby.* For a moment, something inside Lyndell fluttered, and a warm feeling crept through her. She must be crazy to have offered him this, but somehow it made her feel good.

CHAPTER THREE

Jason read his list again. He checked each item—the heat was now off, the hot-water heater was drained, the water pump for the water supply was off, and the circuit breaker was also shut down. He used his flashlight to make his way downstairs. Lyndell said she'd be here by six, and it was just that now.

He hoped she'd be on time, as he was without a jacket or good boots. He saw Duke first as he raced toward him. He braced himself for being toppled, but the dog skidded to a stop at the last second. "Hello, old boy, it's good to see you too."

Lyndell seemed tense as she greeted him. "We have a way to go, so if you're all set, let's start."

Jason nodded. He was about to say, "And a good morning to you too," but kept his wits about him. She must have lots on her mind, and the first was which way to go without meeting many people.

She handed him a small bicycle padlock. "Try this, Jason; it may just keep the door closed, so no animals can get in."

It barely worked, but they had to be satisfied. They covered the door with some branches large enough to deter a closer look.

Lyndell said, "Let's go." She began striding through the woods with a fast but steady pace. Jason kept up, but he was hampered by the cold. When they got toward the road where buses travel, Lyndell stopped and said, "We can get a bus at the next corner that will take us to Walmart. I have a muzzle for Duke, so he can go on the bus too."

When they got to the bus stop, she opened her backpack and took out a muzzle. Duke whined a little, but she patted him and cooed, "Good boy." He sat and gave her his paw.

Lyndell handed Jason some coins that would cover the fare. When the bus arrived, the driver looked at the dog and said, "I ought to charge him double as he's so big." As it is, he rides free. Duke wagged his tail and followed Jason and Lyndell into the bus.

They sat at the back, and he heard her whisper, "I bought a newspaper for you to hide behind. Here, get interested, and don't look up."

He gave her a look that said it all. She giggled. "It isn't often I get to boss a man around. Let me have some fun."

When they reached the store, Lyndell said, "I will give you the money, Jason, and you go and get the things you need. I can stay here with Duke, as he would have to stay muzzled if we took him inside. Do your best to get everything right as we can't exchange them, and be as fast as you can. I hope to be on the bus west by noon—at the latest."

Jason nodded and took the wad of bills she handed to him. He went inside and counted the money. He daren't go over that amount, as he didn't have a penny of his own.

He hurried to the men's aisle and quickly put socks, underwear, two shirts, a pair of jeans, and a warm jacket into the shopping cart. The last was a pair of warm boots. They were likely to be walking in snow or rain for some time, so they had to be waterproof. He had a hard time finding a pair that fit and were not too expensive. When he found a pair, he totaled the items in his head. He had five dollars left over, and he breathed a sigh of relief. He had not figured in the tax, though, and after paying that, he had four cents left.

He took his clothes into a changing room and was happy that everything fit. Now he would be warm and dry, ready for this adventure. His grin was a happy, grateful one.

At the bus stop, Lyndell handed Jason some coins and said, "Here's the money for the ticket. Ask for a transfer, in case we need one. I think this bus takes us close to the Greyhound terminal, but I'm not sure." Jason nodded, and soon, they were on board and seated toward the back.

Jason turned to Lyndell and said, "Lyndell, I can't tell you how much I appreciate what you are doing for me." He put his arms around her to give her a hug.

She pushed him away. "Don't touch me, Jason," she said. Her voice was hard as steel.

"I'm sorry, Lyndell. I meant no harm. Saying thank you was all I intended."

"Well, don't ever touch me again."

Her voice was tense and a little frightened. Jason sat back in surprise. "I said I'm sorry. I'll remember from now on."

Lyndell looked out the window. "Here we are almost at the station," she mumbled. "I will feel better once we are out of Vermont."

They arrived at the station and were soon walking toward it. They both were looking around to see if they were safe. Lyndell said, "Jason, I will go in and get the tickets. You stay with Duke. I will clear his riding on the bus by telling them that he will be muzzled and that I also have a slight vision problem. I hope it works. I don't like to lie, but I have to if we are to get out of here. I don't want us to be seen together yet, so take Duke for a walk close by. I think it will be safe enough."

Jason was anxious as he walked Duke. He kept a lookout for anyone looking like a police officer or his uncle Tomas. So far, all was clear. Like Lyndell, he would be glad to be on their way.

It seemed like hours but was only twenty minutes when Lyndell hurried to him. "I got Duke cleared and two tickets to Glens Falls, New York. I was in that area with my mother before we moved to Vermont. I think I can get a job for a few days. We need to get enough money for a ticket to the next large town and a place to sleep."

Jason nodded in relief when they were on board the bus and it began its way toward the New York border.

Jason closed his eyes and thought about her reaction to his hug. *I seem to be back in her good graces for now. I wonder what has made her so scared of men. It must be something pretty bad to have made her leave home and want to keep her distance from men ... I'll have to be careful not to upset her. Whatever it was, I will do my best to help her. Not all men are like her stepfather.*

For a while, Lyndell sat tense and withdrawn. *Have I overreacted? He meant me no harm. I do think he is a good person. But I can't let him get too close. Even though he is young, he's a man after all.*

She was aware of how drowsy she was and did nothing as she felt Jason gently put her head on his shoulder. Feeling safe, she closed her eyes and let the rhythm of the bus soothe her to sleep …

Jason and Duke kept watch over her until they arrived at a comfort stop. Hoping she would not awake, he carefully removed her head from his shoulder. *No use starting that again*, he thought.

"At the next stop, we'll grab a bite and walk and feed Duke." Jason just nodded. He mentally began to add up all that she spent so far. He had no job and no prospects and was running from the law. Damn. He had to do his utmost to pay her back as soon as possible.

The bus rolled by several fields, still snow covered. He noted small communities with clusters of homes and small farms. Winter in Vermont for farmers was tough. It took stamina and lots of courage to keep at it. It is with pride a man says, "I'm a Vermonter."

Jason was not aware that he dozed off. Lyndell felt him settle her head on his shoulder and smiled at the warm feelings. No, Jason was not like her stepfather or HIM. But still she meant to keep her distance. Her eyes too closed in sleep.

Lyndell opened her eyes. She moved slowly so as not to waken Jason. She took out her money clip. She counted the bills and found that they had enough money for two dinners and one room, probably not a two-bed one at that.

Oh no. We can't share a bed. We just can't. He'll have to sleep on the floor. I'll ask for extra blankets and a pillow. I've got to get a job for the dinner shift for tonight and hopefully a breakfast job for tomorrow. We sure do need money. Maybe Jason can find work too. Her eyes closed as she sighed. Soon she was fast asleep again.

She felt Duke's growl before she heard it. She opened her eyes a fraction and saw a rough-looking man reaching over her to get at her backpack.

"Touch the blue or navy one and you will be on the floor. Believe me, my dog is not a poodle."

"Awe, he's muzzled. He can't hurt me. Besides, these are my backpacks."

"One word from me and you will be on the floor. I'd hate to accidentally loosen his muzzle."

He stood still for a moment. Was she serious? Duke growled again—a warning growl. "Okay, I've made a mistake." He turned and stumbled toward the front of the bus. Lyndell patted Duke's head and said, "Good boy. Thank you, old pal."

The pale winter sun made its way toward the hills. Jason and Lyndell were both awake as they pulled into the bus depot. "I'll walk Duke while you go in and ask if there's a large truck stop near here. Ask if it has a restaurant too. I want to find work if possible."

"Okay, Lyndell. I'll find out how far it is as well."

Lyndell waved as she took Duke's muzzle off. He began to run with her, keeping a modest pace. Jason watched them. *They must have done this a hundred times,* he thought. He admired her slim but curvy body and her easy grace as she ran. Her hair, a brown halo, was tousled by the wind. They both kept a steady rhythm as they took the measure of the parking lot.

Jason beckoned to the bus driver. Jason introduced himself. Then he said, "My friend and I are looking for work, even if it is just for a few days. Do you know of any restaurant or a truck stop nearby? We also are looking for a motel."

"Yes, I know of several restaurants and a truck stop about a mile up this road. I know of two motels that are not far as well. They may need a waitress at this time of the year, and there may be a job as shower room attendant for you. No one likes the shower attendant's job; some men can be obnoxious." Jason thanked him with a smile and a wave.

Jason thought of Duke and decided to keep him with him if he took the job. It would be good insurance, he thought. Duke seemed to obey him just as well as he did Lyndell. The dog had given him his trust, a thought that made Jason very relieved.

Jason saw Lyndell walking toward him with Duke by her side. Lyndell's face was pink from the cool air, and Jason thought she looked beautiful. He wanted to kiss her and hold her. He had to turn away from giving in to his desires.

"Lyndell, the bus driver was very nice. He told me about a restaurant at a truck stop. It is about a mile away. He also said there were several motels and other restaurants close by. There may even be a job for me as a shower attendant. If I get the attendant's job, can I keep Duke with me? The driver said the job had its share of problems with mean men."

She only hesitated a second before saying, "Of course, Jason. He's now your dog too. That means when you walk him, you also clean up. I have some paper bags in my backpack for just that." She grinned evilly at the thought.

CHAPTER FOUR

At the truck stop, Lyndell and Jason were given disappointing news. There were no jobs to be had at this truck stop. But they were told of an Italian restaurant in town that needed a waitress. They decided to try their luck there.

It was a longer walk this time, but when they arrived, they were told there were several waitress jobs open and one waiter's position. They looked around the foyer and were impressed with the decor and the manager's attitude. He gave them a brief interview, and they both had a job for the next day. They were to do the lunch shift—eleven o'clock until two—and the dinner shift. The dinner hours were from four until nine. The manager assumed Jason could wait tables too, and Lyndell decided to keep mum and teach him.

Lyndell asked Jason if he would like to eat there. They would get a 25 percent discount on their dinner. That way, she could fill him in on what a good waiter or waitress did. He nodded, and they found a table close to the kitchen. Lyndell got pencil and paper from her backpack so Jason could take notes.

Duke patiently waited in the vestibule with his muzzle on while they had dinner. The food was excellent, and Jason took lots of mental notes as he observed their waitress and tried to listen to Lyndell at the same time. His head was reeling, but he thought he could do a good job if Lyndell was there to help him.

It was dark when they finally left the restaurant. Jason had seen two motel signs earlier, and they headed toward that area. One was not far from the restaurant and had a vacancy sign lit up outside.

"Jason, would you walk Duke for a little bit while I go talk to the manager? Take a paper bag for Duke's deposits," she said with a grin. He nodded and took Duke's lead. He got several bags out of her backpack and put them into his own. He thought of that grin and wanted to kiss her dizzy.

Lyndell went in to talk to the motel manager. She explained about her slight vision problem and said the dog would be muzzled going in and out of the motel. George, the manager, said he had no problem with that.

The big problem was that there was only one room left, and it had one queen-size bed. Lyndell pondered that and finally agreed to take it. Jason could sleep on the floor.
Thank God there was a job for tomorrow, she thought, as she handed over her last stash of bills.

Lyndell looked around the motel room. It was the usual standard motel room: clean, neat, but sterile. She hurried to take a shower before Jason came back. If she was in bed, in the center, he'd get the message, or maybe not. She snuggled down into the blankets and closed her eyes.

Jason came into the motel room, keeping as quiet as possible. He gave Duke a bowl of water and then went into the bathroom. He didn't turn the light on in the bedroom, so he didn't see Lyndell. When he came out, he slowly got into bed on the empty side. However, something was between them. He put his hand out and felt Duke's head on her pillow. He grinned. *So, she had found a chaperone. I hope Duke doesn't snore.*

There was nothing for breakfast, but they knew if they arrived by ten thirty, there would be something they could nibble on. Jason listened to Lyndell again as she told him the best waiter routine. She was a good teacher, he thought. Somehow he felt able to cope. His confidence level was right up there.

They got paid at the end of the day and between them had enough for another night at the motel and food for a few days. They planned their route west and found that with jobs here and there, it would be about ten days or more until they reached Seattle.

"What are your plans when we get there, Jason?" Lyndell asked.

"Try to see the head of admissions," he replied. "I want to know if they ever sent a reply to my application. I should have at least received an answer, even if they were unable to place me this semester."

"You could have placed a long-distance call to them. Why didn't you?"

"My uncle was breathing down my back, and every move I made was noted. I couldn't take a chance, once I knew what he was up to."

Lyndell nodded. "We'll go see the head honcho, and you will be able to get in. Well, maybe not this semester, but the next one. In the meanwhile, we work, travel, and save what we can.

"Perhaps somehow we can find a way to expose your uncle's plans and get your inheritance back. We should try to come up with a plan and ask someone to help us."

Jason nodded and knew he found a true friend. Hopefully, they could be more as time went on, but for now, he was one lucky guy.

Lyndell looked at Jason and realized all her fear had gone. He was a kind, caring person. She felt safe and at ease, as if she had known him for a long time. Something inside began to hum—a sweet sound—perhaps the music of love?

CHAPTER FIVE

After a few weeks, a pattern was established. They would work for a week, get enough money for tickets to a city on their westward trek, and work there if they found jobs. Lyndell kept some money aside in case they did not find a job right away. They had good luck though and soon had a little in reserve.

Jason knew he was in trouble when he found he could not get Lyndell out of his mind. When working or riding or just enjoying the day, she was there. Her smile, that dimple, and her sweet personality kept him dreaming of what could not be. She filled his dreams at night—exotic dreams of holding her in his arms and sharing a tender but passionate love.

How can I get through those barriers she has placed between us? Why can't she see how much I care? She must know by now that I would never hurt her. Well, I won't give up trying. She is the best friend I ever had. A warm, caring friendship could lead to love.

When they were about a two-week distance from Seattle, Lyndell had some bad luck. She was carrying a tray of dinners to a table when the busboy came out of the kitchen door in a rush. He used the "in" door instead of the "out" one. She had not expected that and tried to keep her balance as she juggled the tray. As she fell, Jason being close by grabbed the tray of food just in time.

Lyndell fell to one side and twisted her ankle. Jason knew she was in real pain. He quickly called Jeff, the manager, and explained what had happened. Within minutes, she was on her way to the emergency room at the local hospital.

The doctor, Aaron Kendall, who was in charge of emergencies, examined Lyndell and then had X-rays taken. "It is a sprain and can be very painful. You'll have to stay off of that foot for about a week." His voice was cold and condescending. Lyndell could almost feel his distaste in his voice.

Jason kept his voice pleasant but firm. "Dr. Kenyon, we are here for only a few days. We have jobs and can pay our way under the usual circumstances. Lyndell got hurt at the restaurant where we are working. They have agreed to pay for the expenses here at the hospital. We are not vagrants who don't want to pay their way." Jason stood and looked at the doctor. His voice had been firm, but his attitude was not combative.

"I am afraid I forget that I was young once," Dr. Kendall said. "I judged you too quickly. I apologize. Now that I understand, I can help you with some crutches, extra salve, and pain medicine. I will also get you a ride back to the restaurant for food and then to your motel." He shook both their hands and wished them good luck.

When they were ready to leave, they were given a pair of crutches, some extra salve, and a warm handshake. An attendant was ready to drive them to the restaurant and then to their motel.

At the restaurant, Jason offered to waitress half of Lyndell's tables until she was better. "That's good news," Jeff said with relief. "I had visions of no waitstaff and this being a Friday. I appreciate your help. Because the accident happened here, I'll add some extra money to your check."

"Thank you," Jason said. "I'll be in tomorrow about ten thirty and then at four." The manager again apologized for the accident and wished Lyndell a good night.

Jason asked for two take-out dinners and some hamburger for Duke. He kept talking to Lyndell on the ride back to their motel, hoping she would relax and be more comfortable. He knew she wasn't only tired but discouraged as well. "Look, Lyndell, I'll take Duke for a walk, feed and water him, and then see about heating our dinner. Okay?"

Jason helped Lyndell into their motel room. She grunted with the pain. Jason helped her sit in the only comfortable chair. Jason made a footstool out of an overturned wastebasket. He gently put her foot up. He gave her two pain pills and a glass of water. She closed her eyes and tried to relax.

After walking Duke and feeding him, Jason began fixing their dinner. It was a salad and some sliced chicken along with Italian bread and butter. There was hot coffee and a slice of lemon pie. Lyndell ate as much as she could and felt much more cheerful.

When they were finished, Jason decided to take a no-nonsense approach to the situation. "Lyndell, I don't want any bull from you. I am going to help you in and out of the shower, help you soak your ankle, put on the salve the doctor gave me, and bandage your ankle. Then you are going to get into bed and rest until the sun is up. I want to help you. I am not here to molest you. Got it?"

She surprised both of them by nodding her head. If he had been looking at her face, he would have seen that dimple as she hid her smile.

By the time he was ready for bed, she was fast asleep. Duke lay beside her and kept one eye on Jason as he slid under the covers. He heard Duke's sigh. Soon, the day's excitement took its toll, and Jason too was fast sleep.

The weeks passed slowly, but at last, Lyndell was walking without pain. "Jason, I think I am ready to go back to work. If we are lucky, we can leave here by next Friday. Look, we have money for our motel room and a lot toward our bus fare.

"Thanks for everything you've done for me, Jason. I know I couldn't have managed without you." Her dimple came and went so quickly, Jason almost missed it. "I think we're even now, and you don't owe me a thing."

They agreed to give Jeff a week's notice that they were going to leave. They had liked working for him and wanted to be fair. They both were happy to have had some time between bus rides for a while.

They agreed to give George, the motel manager, twenty-five dollars for the loan of the recliner. It had been heaven to be able to put her feet up and even sleep in the chair several times.

As they left for the bus terminal, Jason's spirits were high. He felt that Lyndell trusted him more, and even though she still kept him at a distance, he knew he was not going to give up trying to make her love him. *I love her sweet smile, her scent that intrigues me. She has so much courage and a will to succeed. She puts her energy into every effort to overcome her past. I've fallen in love with my lovely friend. It's hell to stay cool and not show her how much I want her to be mine completely. But I know if I am to keep her trust, I have to honor her wishes. Maybe someday soon ...*

Lyndell sat on the edge of the bed and said a mental goodbye to the motel. They had weathered her accident and had a few extra dollars to rely on. They would be traveling for two days, the first a whole day and the next a half day. She hoped they would find a motel with twin beds. She glanced at Duke sprawled out on the carpet. When they got to a city, she should take him for a grooming. When she looked in the mirror and saw herself, she almost laughed. She was the one who needed a makeover.

For several weeks, she found herself wanting to touch Jason. She had never wanted to explore Jason's body until now. When she had taken a peek several times as he was getting into bed, he looked handsome to her. His body was firm with fine dark hairs on his chest and arms. *I know he is strong because he lifted me several times when my ankle hurt. When I look into his blue-green eyes, I see humor lurking there, as well as kindness. I wonder how it would feel to be kissed by him.* A shiver made her heart beat faster, and a longing spread through her that made her breathless.

She knew that all men were not evil or hurtful. Jason had proven he was a kind, caring person. She often studied him when he was not looking. Her heart would beat faster, and a yearning she had never felt before made her feel warm all over.

Whoa, I'd better be careful or I'll be in deep trouble. With my past, keeping my distance is the best thing to do.

As the bus rolled westward, Jason looked at Lyndell. He had promised himself that he would learn more about her. "Lyndell, do you feel that you can trust me enough to confide in me? I have told you all about me, even that my uncle wants to put me in jail, swearing I am a thief. Come on, Lyndell, I'm your friend and want to help all I can."

Her heart raced. She sat quietly until it was normal again. He was being fair. He deserved to know about her family and what had caused her to run away. "Yes, Jason, you do deserve to hear my story. I know you are a friend—a very special one. I have never had a close friend before. After my mom died, my stepfather, Stanly Nickerson, made me come home right from school and do homework and chores. I had to make dinner and clean up too. I was so tired, I went to bed early.

"As I grew older, say thirteen and fourteen, he tried to hug me and kiss me. He always reeked of alcohol. I had to try hard not to vomit. I knew from experience that if I made him angry, he would slap me around.

"One day, when I was sixteen, my mother's attorney, Martha Steinbeck, came to see my stepfather. She explained that a paper had been overlooked that was a codicil to her will. It said that if I married before reaching eighteen, I would get my inheritance then instead of later.

"'Yeah, yeah,' my stepfather yelled. 'I got me a gold mine here.'

"I stared at him in horror. I felt so dizzy; I had to hold on to the sink for balance.

"I remember thinking, does he believe I would marry my drunk of a stepfather? He must be mad. He would make a psychologist weep.

"He grabbed his bottle from the cupboard and took down two glasses. He poured whisky into both and pushed one at me. I shook my head, and he took both glasses into the living room and called his friend Gabby. I could hear a part of what he said, and it seemed they were talking nonstop, planning something, and my stepfather was laughing like an idiot.

"I was really afraid of Gabby Pierce. He was about forty years old, growing bald, had a potbelly and a constant sly look on his face. He always smelled of beer. When he came to our house, my stepfather always said, 'Don't I have a pretty daughter?' It used to make me want to hit him. I was so glad I was not his daughter.

"One day, after we had our dinner, I was washing the dishes when I felt Gabby near me. He had come up behind me and said, "You sweet thang, you, I want to have you right here.'

"Then he quickly put his hands up under my dress. I screamed at him, 'Get away from me, you filthy man!' and I tried to kick him.

"He laughed and pinched me hard. I filled the dishcloth with the soapy water and threw it in his face. He yelled and dropped his hands. I ran as fast as I could out the door and into the street. Luckily, I saw a neighbor and asked if I could walk with her. She looked at me strangely but nodded.

"When I saw my stepfather later, I looked him in the eye and said, 'If Gabby ever touches me again, I will break every bottle of yours that I can find. I will also go to the police and tell them what a dan-dan dandy of a stepfather you are. You understand?' He nodded.

"I turned to put the bottle back in the cupboard when he leaped out of his chair toward me. I grabbed the bottle again and said, 'This time I'll go to the police, and even higher, if I have to.' He glared at me but went out of the house. I knew I couldn't win. He was bigger than me, stronger, and the police would not listen to me anyway. They never had."

Jason squeezed her hand and said, "Why don't you rest awhile. The story can wait. You are exhausted."

Lyndell nodded, and soon her eyes closed. Jason was pleased that she kept her hand in his. Her trust in him made him vow again to protect her and shield her from danger.

When they arrived at the next rest stop, Lyndell was surprised at how free she felt. Confiding in Jason and sharing her troubles were a relief. Her look was almost one of love, he thought. They went for a walk together, holding hands. He helped her back into the bus, and soon, they were on their way westward again.

"Lyndell, what happened after that? Did Gabby stay away?"

"Well, for a while he did, but when he was around, I was careful to stay well away from him. It was about two months later when I overheard my stepfather talking with Gabby. I moved closer to the living room door so I could hear what they were saying.

"'We can't wait much longer 'cause I am running out of money. I can't find a job right now, and soon, I'll be unable to buy food, or whisky, let alone pay the mortgage.'

"Gabby said, 'Well, what are you waiting for? If we scare her enough, she'll do what we say. We can be hitched in no time, and the money will be ours—well, mine, but of course, we're partners.'

"My stepfather, Stanly, sat thinking for a few minutes. Then he replied, 'We can go to the courthouse and get a marriage license. I know of a girl who would go with us and pretend to be Lyndell. She's the same build and hair color. She could be a twin to Lyndell.

"'When we get to the justice of peace, he'll never know the difference, and Lyndell will be cranked up on some stuff I have that will make her docile.'

"'Sounds great to me. When do we do it?'

"'How about Friday?' my stepfather asked. 'Then you two can have a weekend honeymoon.' His laugh was almost diabolical.

"I tiptoed to the stairs and went to my room. I checked my money, a few dollars that I had stashed away from babysitting a few times. I had twenty dollars and some change. I thought of the place where I had seen my stepfather hide money. I listened to hear if they were still talking. They were, so I took a chance and went into the bathroom off of his room. In the medicine closet, I found the pouch. I took it all, not even counting it. I held my breath and silently crept back to my room.

"I found my school backpack and stashed some clothes, a second pair of heavy shoes, and the money. I waited until I knew the men had gone out and then put some bottled water, luncheon meat, and cheese in the bag. I dressed warmly. I thought to take some matches and a flashlight.

"Looking around for the last time, I knew I had no place to go, but leaving the place was the best idea I had. I thought of my mom and almost cried at the feeling of loss and of how much I missed her.

"I walked and ran for the rest of the day. I hoped to reach the lake before dark. I tried to keep away from busy roads, and when I saw the lake, I recalled a cottage I once knew as a young girl. My mother had a friend who owned a cottage by the lake. I looked until I felt certain it was the right one and got inside, after some hard work. I had been there several days when I knew someone was close by.

"So that's my story. If I can get money enough, I'll go back and see my stepfather in jail or die trying. He not only abused me but has taken my inheritance as well."

Jason turned and kissed her on her forehead. He sat still and held her close until his rage subsided. He had never felt an urge to beat someone senseless before, but he knew he'd like to take on Lyndell's stepfather, Stanly, and Gabby. That would put him in jail for good, he thought. But it might just be worth it.

He thought about all she had told him. Evidently, her stepfather, Stanly, had once been a good citizen. He was respected and admired. It was only after his wife died that he began to drink heavily. Now, he'd lost his job and could barely pay his bills. His one good friend was an alcoholic but still respected in the town. Lyndell was right. No one would believe her. There had been no witnesses to back up Lyndell's story, and any bruises were now gone.

The best thing I can do is just stay close to her. If things get too sticky, there is one way out. We can get married, and then she would have my protection as well as her inheritance. She won't like it, but a marriage of convenience would solve her problems, and she could later obtain a divorce or annulment. That would probably take more trust than she has to give. But then what is the alternative? Go back to her home and dear old stepdaddy?

He breathed a sigh of relief at the thought of helping her. He knew he more than admired her. It was more, much more. She was in all his thoughts and dreams. Now, if he could convince her to marry him—then maybe? It was a nice daydream.

CHAPTER SIX

Weary of sitting and riding, they welcomed a motel in the next city. Jason looked around the room. It had two beds and looked almost homey. Lyndell agreed that they had enough money to stay two days and rest up.

There was a park across the road that appealed to Lyndell, and she soon was headed out with Duke for a little exercise. Jason followed along and was surprised to see Lyndell going through commands for Duke.

He responded instantly, even crawling on his belly when she said, "Sneak up and don't run."

"How long have you had Duke, Lyndell?"

"Not long at all. It's been only since I ran away from Stanly and Gabby. He found me as I was running toward the woods and has been my shadow ever since. When I saw him running beside me, I was scared. At first, I thought he was a police dog or perhaps Stanly sent a dog to track me down.

"I don't know who he belongs to or where he came from. He just took me under his wing, so to speak, and I am protected."

"Wow! What a gift. You are both lucky. You take good care of him, and he returns the favor."

"If I were a superstitious person, I would think he was sent to me. But I guess that's nonsense, isn't it?"

"Not really. Lots of strange things happen in this world that can't be explained. Duke seems to have a mission to guard you. He does it well too. He won't let anyone hurt you, if he's beside you."

"The first day, after leaving my home, I was nearing the cottages when I saw a man in the distance. He was looking at me too. As he came closer, I stopped. He kept on coming, and suddenly, Duke gave a huge snarl. His back hair went up, and he kept on showing his teeth and growling. The man jumped a little, turned, and walked away as fast as possible in the snow. I whispered, 'Good dog. Good boy.' Duke gave me his paw, and I heard a low sound that I imagined was his way of saying, 'You're welcome.'"

"You know, Lyndell, I think Duke likes me too and would protect me also."

"I know he would, Jason. We are a team now. The three of us off to Washington State."

The next morning after breakfast, Lyndell asked Jason about his plans. He said he'd tell her all about them, but first, he wanted to walk a bit. He had seen an amusement park in the distance and wanted to check it out.

She nodded and said, "Can I come too? I'd like a walk and see the park and what the amusements are like. It will not be operating now, as it's still cold weather."

When they got to the park, they found a merry-go-round that was not covered, and Jason helped Lyndell up on one of the horses.

"Lyndell, I am not certain yet what courses I have to take to get a diploma in oceanography. I've already had lots of math, which is important and required. I need more science courses and specialized ones. I know it will take several years to complete them, but I know I will make the grade. The last year of college sounds fantastic with me diving down under the surface in a special small submarine and seeing what is beneath the waves."

"Jason, why do you want to do all this studying? What is so appealing about the ocean?"

"Oh, lots of things. For one, the ocean has always been a mystery to me. How large are the oceans? How is it possible to have underground volcanoes? What is the Sargasso Sea? And of course, much more.

"There are strange-colored and odd-looking fish. Fish that glow in the dark, and fish that have a way of communicating with each other. I heard there is a pool of fresh water under the surface in places. Why? I want to learn it all. I also know if we don't free our oceans of garbage, other cast-off pieces of debris and plastic, our fish, which we all depend upon for food, will die."

Lyndell sat quietly for a moment. All he had said was new to her. She didn't know about the pollution of the ocean waters. If the fish sickened and died, the world's food supply would diminish. Starvation would be common, and it would be too late to change things.

"Why didn't I know about this? I've heard a little over the TV, but not a lot. Perhaps it isn't newsworthy as yet. Sometimes it takes something catastrophic to wake us up.

"Jason, what can you do to help clean up the ocean and prevent it from becoming worse? You are only one person after all."

"Well, for starters, I can help educate by teaching, making videos, and so forth. But first, I need the skills to do that. I can also educate people about family planning. The world is overpopulated, but you can't make people become good shepherds of the earth with laws. It has been tried, and it failed. We must want to care for our world—its lands and its oceans. That will take a miracle, but I hope it can be done. It must if we are to survive here on earth. "All of it is still here today—all of the greed, lust for power, and the religious dogma that goes back to the back of beyond. But we must try to make people see the dangers ahead. Humanity's future is going to depend on us. All it takes is common sense and a will to work for what's best for the earth and humanity."

"Oh, Jason, I hope you can see your dream come true. One dedicated person can make a difference."

"Thanks, Lyn. I'm going to do my best. I know that many others feel the same way. And every one of us counts. So I am not the 'Lone Ranger.'" He grinned and put his arm around her. She did not cringe or pull away. *Well, there's a little hope at last.*

"Lyn, what are your plans for your future? Would you like to learn a skill? You could take courses to be a nurse or an office manager or a teacher's aide."

She sat pensive for a moment before replying. "I don't even have a few skills to start with. I have not finished the eleventh grade—so, no high school diploma.

"I can type a letter, but I am slow at it. I'm not great on the computer, but I think I could learn. But how? I can't enroll in school without a home base. I have no job prospects—except waitressing."

"Lyndell, I am going to clear my name. Somehow I will find someone to help me. If I can do that, I will be financially secure. Then would you let me help you—as a trusted friend, of course. You must know that I care for you deeply. I want you to be mine, completely, not just for today but always. I also know you are not ready for that. But you can trust me. I can be patient and would never force myself on you. I think I've proved that by now.

"If you would let me care for you, you could work part-time—if you wanted to. Then you could take the courses that will give you your GED. After that, you can choose what courses to take to get the skills you need. I'll leave our future together up to you. Just let me care for you now. You've helped me when I needed you. Let me be there for you."

Jason looked at her and held his breath. She was a vision of beauty to him. Her shiny dark brown hair, her fair skin, and her lovely blue-gray eyes made him want to touch her, hold her, and—no, it was too soon. For now, as her friend, he could help her if she'd let him.

"Oh, Jason, thanks. I appreciate all you have done for me and your offer to do more. But if I can get a good waitress job, I'll be okay. It's good of you to want to provide for me, but I want to be on my own, if possible."

Jason took a deep breath and scowled. He was exasperated, and he scowled. He would like to shake her for being so obstinate. "Being independent is fine if you are not being pursued. Stanly and Gabby will find you, believe me. When they do, I want to be there. I also have a plan B that I am sure will work. Think about what I've just said for a few days, okay?"

"Okay, Jason, I will." She turned away before he could see the tears in her eyes. *He can't really care for me. How can he? I'm just a runaway kid with no social standing, no financial prospects, and I'm scrawny to boot.*

She looked down at her breasts and groaned. *They are so small. I'm not pretty or feminine at all. And God, I can't forget that awful day Gabby came to the house and ... Oh, why can't I forget it? I can never tell Jason. He will turn away in disgust. No decent person will want me, not ever.*

It took all her willpower to keep Jason from seeing how upset she was. If he ever found out what happened that day, it would break her heart as she knew she had begun to love him. She wanted to belong to him completely—body and soul. *It can never be.*

CHAPTER SEVEN

They arrived in Seattle on a rainy, foggy day. After putting on their rain gear, they walked for miles, checking out the town. Their aim was to find the motel section of the city. They both thought it would be close to the ocean and headed in that direction.

They saw a park with some secluded benches and sat down to rest. Duke sat with them and kept checking the area out for strangers. Lyndell counted her money, and with Jason's added, it came to almost $200.

They bought a newspaper and learned some helpful things, especially about prices—which were much higher than they were used to. The restaurant ads gave them several places to start looking for work.

"Let's find out if we can take a bus from here to the downtown area," Jason said. "I think we are both tired, and we can see even more of the city from the bus."

"Good idea. We can look for motels as we go."

After a few blocks, they came to a large intersection. There, they found where the motels were, as well as the restaurants.

From there, they took a bus that passed several large motels and what looked like the top-of-the-line restaurants.

They found a good motel that was not too expensive just as the heavens opened. Rain poured, and they both were soaked in minutes. At the motel, they were greeted with grins and remarks about Seattle's great weather. They were also handed a towel and a welcoming smile.

The room had two beds that were inviting. Jason thought that if they put them together, they would be even better. Jason knew Lyndell did not share this thought. He shrugged. What else was new? God, he had to be a saint. The thought of going to bed with her and not touching her was driving him insane. He needed a cold shower, even if he was already wet.

After dinner and a walk with Duke, Jason sat by the window and stared out. Lyndell noticed that Jason was too quiet. He looked discouraged for the first time in weeks.

"Come on, Jason, you can smile. We are finally here, so what's the problem?"

"Oh, I don't know. I guess I'm thinking that I'm deep in doo-doo. It seems too much, all at once. I have traveled here and don't even know where the college is located. I have little hope of meeting with the person in charge of admissions. I'm broke, and my uncle Tomas is trying to put me in jail. I have every right to be down."

Lyndell took a militant stance. "Jason, I'd like to kick your ass. We've come a long way, and you can't lose your confidence now. You're tired—well, so am I. Take a shower and then to bed. We'll both feel better in the morning. A little sun, a job, and you will see the rainbow. We can do it, Jason. Keep the faith."

Impulsively, she put her arms around him and kissed him. It was a light kiss, but a kiss is a kiss, Jason thought. She drew back and smiled, just a friendly smile. It gave Jason hope and raised his spirits. It also raised something else, and he tried to hide it by turning away. *God knows how I want her. How long can I stand this yearning and her disinterest? If I want to win her, though, I just have to keep protecting her, and maybe a miracle will happen.*

Outside, the sun peeked through the clouds. The rainbow made a show of its colors. Its end was out of sight, but the promise was there. *Yes, I'll keep my dreams and follow the rainbow to the very end.*

The next day, they looked for a more reasonable hotel. They were all the same—they were too expensive for them. They stood dejected and wet on the corner of a busy street in the downtown area.

They looked around for Duke, but he crossed the street and seemed to be waiting for them. When the light turned green, they ran across to Duke, who then turned and trotted up the street. They followed him for several blocks and began to wonder if he had lost his bearings. Where was he taking them?

He stopped at a small brown church and ran up the steps to the big front door. Duke barked several times before the door opened. A silver-haired man with a serene smile beckoned them in.

"I wondered who my visitors would be today, and here are two, almost drowned, angels. Come in and welcome." He led the way inside and toward the back of the church.

"I have a little sanctuary where I can make tea. I also have some Oreo cookies for you." He opened a door to a neat room that held a small stove, refrigerator, and sink.

"Take off your rain gear, and dry off a little." He tossed them a towel. "Then have a seat. I'll hang up your things to dry out a bit."

They did as he suggested and then sat in one of the inviting chairs with a contented sigh. Lyndell looked around the room and found it neat and tidy for a lone man. There was a small table on which rested some cups and plates. She watched as he set out some Oreo cookies and two dog treats.

When the tea was ready, he said, "My name is Gregg Johnson, and I'm the minister of this Wayside Chapel. What are your names, and how may I help you?"

Lyndell and Jason both spoke at once. They stopped and laughed, finished drying off, and gave the towel to Reverend Johnson.

"My name is Lyndell Cordell, and I'm from Essex, Vermont."

Jason spoke next and said his name was Jason Weston and was from Colchester, Vermont.

"Lyndell and Jason are nice names, and I hope you are ready for some tea."

He handed a cup to Lyndell and one to Jason. He offered them the plate of cookies, and after they had taken some, he gave the milk bone to Duke, who wolfed it down in a flash.

"Now, how may I help you? I sense I have two strangers to Seattle, low on funds, and in need of some fatherly advice. Am I right?"

Once Lyndell began, it all poured out—her home life, her stepfather, her fear of Gabby, and the events leading to this moment. "Good lord, girl, I'm glad you're here. You need some good advice, not just sympathy."

He turned to Jason. "Can you tell me your story now?"

As Jason began, he thought the reverend would never believe him. He was not aware of how his sincerity and quiet confidence convinced Reverend Johnson of the truth. There was a moment of silence when Jason finished. The only movement was from Duke, who stood and looked longingly at the bone still on the plate.

"Oh my, how could I forget your four-legged friend?" He gave the treat to Duke, who gently took the bone from the man's hand. It was gone in a second.

"I believe you need someplace to stay for a few days where you will feel secure. Am I right?" They both nodded. "There is a Mission House close by where you may be able to stay for a week or so, if they are not full. I will speak to the administrator, Rosa, but I'm sure she will agree to your stay. You will have two meals a day and time during the day to seek out the person at the college you want to meet. There won't be a charge, but it would be a blessing if you could help with meal preparation and some cleaning up. Would that be an answer to your problems for now?"

Jason had an incredible look on his face. "Oh yes! I can't believe it. You are a godsend." He laughed at what he'd said. "Well, you are, Reverend Johnson. No pun intended."

Reverend Johnson had a serene smile as he shook their hands. "I'm happy to know that you believe the solution is God sent. Shall we have a moment of prayer?" They all bowed their heads, except for Duke. He was busy eying the empty plate.

Reverend Johnson gave them a note to the administrator of the Mission House. He also gave them directions and described the house to them. It was not far, and they could walk there. With grateful thanks, they began the walk.

CHAPTER EIGHT

They stood in front of the Mission House and were in awe of its fine architecture. It was a two-story building made of soft tan-colored stone. There were several add-ons, but they did not detract from the building at all. Jason noted that the grass needed some more work and thought he could do something about that, if they could stay.

"Well, Lyndell, it's now or never." He took her hand, and they were soon at the front door. "Stay, Duke. Hide for a while." The dog disappeared into the bushes and sat dawn.

The petite lady who answered their knock was either Spanish or Mexican. Her soft brown eyes held a smile of welcome. She took the note that Reverend Johnson had given them and said, "My name is Rosa Rodriquez. I am the administrator here. Please come inside and get dry and warm. Then you can tell me why you need to be here.

"How is Reverend Johnson? I hope he is well."

"He seemed in good health to me," Lyndell replied. "Perhaps just a little tired."

Rosa nodded her head. "It is always the same. He keeps too busy these days. He just won't slow down no matter how much we scold him."

When they were dry and warm, Rosa gave them a tour of the house, along with some special rules. When she asked if they had eaten breakfast, they shyly said no. She gave them each a banana and a glass of milk. "I hope that will do until dinner, which is about six.

"I have one room left for tonight. If you can share, it is fine with me. Tomorrow there may be a larger room with twin beds. I can't promise that, but we'll manage someway."

"Thank you, Rosa. I am happy that you have room for us," Jason said.

They went into the living room and sat in comfortable chairs. Rosa then told them more about the Mission House and the other guests. At one point, she cocked her head. "What is that odd noise I hear? Where is it coming from? It sounds as if it is right below the window."

Lyndell took a deep breath and began explaining about Duke. "Duke is a very special dog, Rosa. He has guarded Jason and me for almost two months. He is quiet, clean, and gentle. May we keep him if we promise to care for his needs?" She held her breath.

"I wondered how long it would take to let me know about Duke. Reverend Johnson appealed to me to bend the rules just for this once as he thought the dog was your partner. I know you can't abandon him now that you are all here in Seattle."

Jason and Lyndell gasped in shock. "Thank you, Rosa. You don't know how much this means to us."

"Well, let me see this paragon. I hope he will not frighten the children here."

Jason went to the front door and called Duke's name. He was inside and shaking himself before Jason could say a word. Rosa appeared with a large towel, and soon, Duke was his old glossy self. He sat and offered his paw to Rosa, showing off his gentle, kind personality. She laughed. "Well trained, are you? Welcome to the Mission House.

"I've got to start dinner preparations now," Rosa said. She rose. "We are having meat loaf tonight."

"May we help with the preparations?" Lyndell asked.

Rosa seemed surprised but readily agreed she could use the help. In the kitchen, Jason began chopping onions, peppers, and garlic. Lyndell began to make a chocolate pudding and then asked if she could do the salad.

Rosa gave a grateful sigh. She sat and rested her feet on a footstool. "Thanks for all your help today. I'm finished early and can rest a few more minutes before setting the table."

"Stay where you are, Rosa," Jason said. "I am the best table setter in the world. Just tell me for how many, and voila, it will be done."

"Please set it for twelve, and if Duke can have some meat loaf, give him some before anyone gets here. I know you don't have extra food for him tonight. And he's part of the family now."

Jason nodded his thanks and went to the kitchen to set out the plates and silverware for the meal.

It was a diverse group that gathered for dinner. They did not mind Duke at all, and the little ones hugged him until he pretended sleep for some peace. They said their good-byes, and a few stayed to clear the table and help with washing up. Rosa, wishing everyone a "good night," went to her room soon after that. There were three women who were sleeping there, and they went up early. They said they had a long day.

After setting the table for breakfast, Lyndell and Jason went up to their room. Jason eyed the bed and said, "Do you think we are getting a message here?"

Her "No!" was loud and clear, and her look would have cooled a randy teen.

Jason shrugged but then winked at her. He knew she was not afraid of him anymore. Also, he had seen a spark of desire in her eyes several times when she looked at him. *Patience, Jason, patience.* His smile seemed to baffle her, and she went into the bathroom to hide her turbulent feelings.

The days added up until three weeks had gone by. They looked for jobs, but since there were so many young people looking for work, they had no offers. Jason kept trying to get an appointment with the head of admissions without any luck. They kept busy between times helping out at the Mission House. It was beginning to feel like home to them, although he knew that time was running out. They could not stay there forever.

April brought some sunny days. Jason had cut the grass, weeded the flower beds, and did some caulking of windows. Rosa appreciated all this, but Jason knew they had to find a solution to their problems soon.

"It's a great day for the beach, Lyndell. Why don't we pack a lunch, if it's okay with Rosa, and go to Houghton Beach Park. We can enjoy the sand and sun for a while."

Surprised, Lyndell agreed. She hadn't seen anything of her stepfather, Stanly, so she felt secure. "That's really nice, Jason. I'll help get the food ready while you fix Duke some food and water. His muzzle is in my backpack."

At the beach, the sun sparkled on the water. The warm sand felt good to Lyndell, and she sat down on the blanket Jason had spread for her. Rosa had given them the blanket, an old one. She'd said, "It's just right for the beach."

Lyndell stared at the water for a while. It was so vast, so blue green, with sunlight sparkling off each wave. They splashed and ducked and tried to swim for a while, but the undertow was tiring.

They enjoyed their lunch of leftover salad and some apples. Duke wolfed his lunch down and lapped up the water in his bowl. He chased waves for a long time and finally grew tired and lay down beside Lyndell.

"Lyndell, I'm going to walk a little way down the beach. There doesn't seem to be anyone along that stretch. I won't be long. Keep Duke with you, okay? Maybe you can even take a nap."

As Jason ambled up the beach, he thought he saw in the distance a small toddler coming toward him. There didn't seem to be anyone else close by. He watched as the child took a few steps and then sat down with a plop.

As the child got close, he could tell it was a girl. She wore a bathing suit that was the same color as the bow in her hair. Determined, she stood again and walked a few more steps until her little feet slipped in the sand.

Jason felt his heart race. *Where are her parents? How could she be on the beach alone? Where was her family?*

The child was still a little away from him when she turned toward the water. *Oh no, don't even think of it!* She stood for only a moment and then leaned to catch a wave, as it rolled onto the beach. She stood and took a few more steps into the water, and Jason began to run toward the child. A large wave made her lose her balance, and the next one pulled her out toward the deep sea.

Jason raced toward her, and when he got close, he plunged into the water. He grabbed for her suit but missed it the first try. A wave came in again and pulled her out of his reach. He glimpsed the bow in her hair and dove again. He finally got her safe in his arms and began to swim toward the beach. He laid her down on her tummy and patted her back until water gushed out. She sputtered and, to Jason, turned almost a blue color. He repeated patting her on her back. When she stopped bringing up water, he held her to him and crooned a little song. She finally stopped shivering, and he said a prayer of thanks.

He heard a shout and looked up and down the beach. He saw a man, waving his hands in the air, as he stumbled along. Jason yelled, "Slow down. She's all right."

He was closer to Jason now, and Jason could see he was an older man, with silver hair. His face was red and his eyes bulging. He started to call out to Jason but then suddenly fell, facedown, on the sandy beach.

Jason laid the child down, as she seemed to be all right for now. He went to the man and, as gently as possible, turned him over on his back. He brushed the sand from his face and checked his heartbeat. It was slow and a little weak but still beating steadily. He looked up and saw Lyndell and Duke racing toward them.

"Lyndell!" yelled Jason. "Bring the cell phone quick!"

She held it up in her hand to show him she had it with her. "Dial 911, Lyndell. Tell them it's a possible heart attack and a nearly drowned child. They both need help. I can't give them our exact location, but it is at Houghton Beach Park and close to a short-stop deli called Scotty's."

It was only a short time until the paramedics came. They quickly took care of the man, and he was soon in the ambulance with all the special care they could give. The little girl was in Jason's arms, and the paramedics asked him to ride with them to the hospital, as the girl did not want to leave him.

"Stay here, Lyndell, with Duke, until I come back. I don't think it will be long. They need me to explain what happened."

She nodded and, as the ambulance rolled away, said a prayer for both of them. What a miracle that Jason had been on the beach and saw the little one in danger. She lay back on the blanket with Duke and closed her eyes. A tear or two rolled down her face, and she sobbed a little. Duke seemed to understand and laid his paw on her leg and gave a woof of sympathy.

What an incredible dog. I wonder who cared for him before he found me. "We are so lucky to have you, Duke. Don't ever leave us."

Duke sighed and looked out to the sea. He gave a little woof and closed his eyes.

CHAPTER NINE

Lyndell tried to relax. She listened to the waves as they rolled ashore. It calmed her a little, and she said another prayer for the little girl and the old man.

She dozed and basked in the sun's warmth. When she woke up, she walked down the beach and then back, afraid she'd miss Jason when he returned. The sun had taken its warmth away and was slowly setting.

What was keeping Jason? She had no sweater and no money for a bus trip back to the Mission House. Just as she was getting anxious about being on the beach in the dark, a car appeared in the distance.

Duke stood and growled, ready to do his job if needed. He gave a happy bark when he saw Jason step out of the Land Rover. A tall, lanky man climbed out of the car and came to Lyndell with an outstretched hand.

"You must be Lyndell. I am sorry to have kept Jason for so long, but the hospital is very thorough, and there is always paperwork. My name is Lloyd Cantile, and I am Roseanne's father, and the man who collapsed is my dad."

"How are your father and Roseanne? Was she able to come home today?"

"Yes. She's with her mother now, and my father is very much improved. Of course, he has to slow down. Making him do that is the big problem. He's stubborn." He laughed. "So am I, I guess.

"I can take you to the Mission House if you are all set to go."

Lyndell sighed. Her relief was obvious. "Thank you very much. I am ready and appreciate your doing this for us."

"Hey, after what you did for my family, I am happy for anything I can do for you."

When they reached the Mission House, Lloyd said goodbye and added, "Roseanne and my father are going to be all right, thanks to you for your quick action. We won't forget this, believe me. You will be hearing from us soon." Jason shrugged aside the thought of being a hero but looked pleased nevertheless.

When Lloyd had gone, Lyndell searched through the food in the refrigerator. Rosa said that she would not be making dinner that night. She found some cheese and a few eggs. There was no bread, but scrambled eggs and cheese made a welcome meal. She also found a few cookies hidden way back in the cub bard.

Jason's eyes were alight with excitement as he related the events of the day. "Lyndell, I can't believe it! When I spoke to Lloyd Cantile, while we waited for news of his dad, he listened to my whole story. He also told me his father, Alan, knows the admissions administrator of Washington State College. His name is Jefferson Wilder. He says he will get me an interview with him as soon as he can.

"Before we left, his father was able to tell us what happened at the beach. He said he was watching Roseanne for the day, as her mom and dad wanted to go to dinner at a new French restaurant. Since he loved to be with her, he agreed to care for her for the day. He thought he had dozed for a minute or two, and when he awoke, he couldn't see Roseanne anywhere. In a panic, he ran up and down the beach, calling her name— nothing. His heart was pounding and his breath short, but he kept on calling her name.

"He said that he ran down the beach again and saw her close to the water's edge. He yelled, but she was far away, and the sea was loud. He saw her try to grab a wave and fall into the water. He saw me run toward her, but she was rolled over by a huge wave. Then I dived into the ocean and, after a moment, brought her out. He said he was now close to them, but his heart was racing and his breath only a faint pant. Then he saw that she was lying on the sand, and the man was doing something—he couldn't see. He felt a pain in his chest and arm and then felt no more.

"At this point, the nurse came in and shooed us away. But we were able to get most of the story, and his dad was able to thank me."

Lyndell listened with wide eyes. "I just can't believe it!" she said over and over. "What a strange day, and what a blessing that Lloyd knows the admissions person. Maybe the age of miracles isn't over after all."

Lyndell gratefully sank into bed. She was so tired. She fell asleep thinking of the way Jason had looked while telling of his chances to meet with the college admissions director.

His face was alive with excitement. His eyes were shining, and his whole stance was one of anticipation. Her heart beat faster. She realized that she loved him. She loved everything about him—his strength, his determination, and his willingness to keep on striving for his goals.

What a good ending, she thought, to a troublesome day. She was almost asleep when little Roseanne's face came clearly to her. She thought how nice it must be to have a child. A boy who looks like Jason? Perhaps someday? Her eyes closed in sleep.

True to his word, Lloyd stopped at the Mission House a week later and told Jason that he had an interview with the admissions director, Jefferson Wilder, on May 4, at nine o'clock. Lloyd offered to take him there in his car and bring him home again. Jason was almost speechless.

"Oh my God! Oh, Lloyd, how can I thank you? This is what I have been working toward for months. I hope he will hear me out as I can't come to classes unless my uncle is exposed as a person who has treated me badly and I can retrieve my inheritance. I am really thankful you have done this for me. Thanks again."

"Well, I am happy to be able to do it. Good luck with the interview." He waved a good-bye and was whistling as he went out the door.

Jason looked at himself in the mirror that hung over the bureau in their bedroom. He had had his hair trimmed, a hot shower, and he wore his favorite shirt. It was a plaid of cream and light green. Lyndell had surprised him and had polished his shoes while he was in the shower. He shrugged and ran his hand through his hair. *I can't do any better with the clothes I've got. I'll have to do.*

He walked into the bedroom to say good-bye to Lyndell. He turned around for her inspection. Then, to her surprise, he gave her a friendly hug. "Wish me well, Lyndell. This is not just for me. It is for you as well." He heard Lloyd's voice downstairs, and he hurried to get going.

The admissions administrator, Jefferson Wilder, was a tall man. He was about fifty years old and had a shock of dark brown hair with some silver streaks in them. He welcomed Jason with a wide smile and gestured for him to take a comfortable-looking armchair that was close to a window. Jason could see flowers and bushes with a birdbath in view.

Jefferson Wilder took a chair close by and said, "This is my favorite view as birds keep me company most of the year—some even in winter."

Jason tried to hide his surprise, as he had thought the interview would be more formal. Jason saw several birds hopping on the rim of the birdbath. He smiled his appreciation.

After a few moments of general conversation, Jason and Jefferson Wilder had achieved a friendly rapport. Jefferson asked Jason to call him by his first name and leave out any formalities. "I know about what happened at the beach. You are a very quick-thinking young man. You helped save two lives and have earned our respect and gratitude.

"Now, Jason, tell me all about the events from the time you sent your application till today. Take your time. I'll listen and ask questions when you are finished."

Jason must have shown his surprise. "Yes, Jason, I want to hear all that your uncle and his lawyer have done to put you in this predicament."

Jason began with his father's death. He explained about the will and how it was set up. He also said that once his father had died, strange things began to happen. He recounted the lack of response from the college, the pictures being taken for "cleaning," the missing expensive animal statues, and the conversation between his uncle and his lawyer. "When I knew what they were planning, I climbed out a window and ran as far as I could before dark."

He then told about meeting Lyndell and the dog, Duke, and their trip by bus to Seattle. He told about how they found the Mission House and how kind Reverend Johnson had been. He did not realize that the director of admissions saw much more than Jason was telling. He smiled to himself, knowing that he would do all he could to help this young man. He was intrigued by his telling about Lyndell and Duke. He loved an adventure, and this was a big one.

When Jason finished telling about his uncle and the problems that brought him here, Jefferson asked him about his reason for wanting to become an oceanographer.

Jason's eyes were clear and lit with anticipation as he gave his reasons for wanting to come to this college. Jefferson paid attention and felt he could help Jason reach his goals. He thought about Jason's problems in Vermont and a way to find out the truth so Jason could have his inheritance restored.

When Jason finished, Jefferson Wilder sat and quietly reviewed all that had been said. Then he told him about his plans to help him. "Jason, would you be agreeable to a plan I have that would help you solve your problems?" Jason nodded and said, "Yes, I would, Mr. Wilder."

"Well, here it is. I have contacts in Vermont that would hire a detective to resolve this problem. He would investigate your uncle Tomas and his attorney. If they find evidence of fraud, tampering with the US mail, and planning to unlawfully accuse you of theft, he can be in jail pronto.

"An attorney would have to be involved at this point. You may also have to appear to give your story. The attorney would represent you. Of course, your uncle will have his day in court. However, if he's found guilty, your trust fund would be yours. If we can find proof of your uncle's trickery, he may confess and seek to plea bargain. Will you agree to my doing this, at no charge to you, until everything is resolved?"

Jason was speechless. He gulped and finally said with a stutter, "I would be forever grateful for all your help. You have given me a gift that I cannot repay. That is your faith and trust in me. If there is anything I can do, let me know."

"Well, for starters, give me your uncle's full name and address. Also, I'd like his business address. Then I need his lawyer's home address and office address as well. It would help to have the shop's address that your uncle sent you to and the name of the policeman who joined your uncle and lawyer in this plan."

When they had settled all the details, Jason left with Lloyd in a state of euphoria. He was walking on clouds and could hardly wait to tell Lyndell. After his good-byes to Lloyd, he went in search of Lyndell. She was nowhere to be found. His letdown was painful, and he sat and worried until he heard her come in the back door.

He swept her off her feet and then gave a hug and a kiss on her forehead. He swung her around and around until she cried, "Oh stop, you are making me dizzy."

He laughed and put her down but still kept his arm around her waist. "Lyndell, I have the best news ever, honest. All our plans are coming true. Jefferson Wilder is going to do all he can to solve my problems. He has a plan that he feels will be the answer. Then when I came toward the Mission House, I saw a rainbow just overhead. I think it means happiness for both of us."

Duke, who had been watching, gave a leap in the air and a happy woof. Jason and Lyndell were so wrapped up in their joy they beamed at each other and did not hear him.

CHAPTER TEN

The next morning, Jason and Lyndell were up and busy by first light. They were grateful to the Mission House for letting them stay there and feeding them. They wanted to repay them in any way they could. They both helped with breakfast and the cleanup. During the day, Lyndell did laundry, and Jason helped to hang the sheets outdoors. Lyndell dusted, kept the kitchen clean, and helped to prepare veggies for dinner.

Jason cut the grass and tended the shrubs and flowers. He also swept the path to the house. He earned money by cutting grass for several neighbors, and he gave this money to the Mission House as part payment for their stay there.

The warm months brought more sunshine, and soon, Lyndell began to blossom. Her face was a warm tan, her eyes bright, and her manner relaxed. She had more confidence, and her bubbling personality became more apparent every day.

The more time she and Jason were together, the more he understood her. Jason loved her more each day. He hoped and prayed she would marry him when his inheritance was restored. He couldn't imagine living without her by his side.

Lyndell knew Jason was giving her loving looks. They made her feel special and caused a tingling feeling deep inside her. She wished she could erase the past and have all the things his eyes promised. Oh damn her miserable stepfather, Stanly, and his buddy, Gabby. What she yearned for could never be. At night, she dreamed of his loving hands caressing her, his words making her long for more, and she squirmed, wanting him, even as she slept.

Jason tried not to be anxious. Weeks had gone by with no news from Jefferson Wilder. He was optimistic one day and in the pits of gloom the next. *What's taking so long? Maybe the investigation will not prove anything, and my uncle Tomas will stay free and keep my inheritance after all.*

So it was a surprise when a call came from Jefferson Wilder, inviting him to come and see him. Jason's heart raced. What if it's bad news? No, it must be good news, or else he wouldn't sound so happy over the phone. He straightened his shoulders. *I have to accept whatever they've found. But God, I hope it is good news.*

The day was fine for Seattle. The sun shone in a clear blue sky. He took the bus to the college and with mixed feelings opened the door to Jefferson Wilder's office. With outstretched hand, Jefferson greeted him, "Good news, Jason, good news indeed. Have a seat, and I'll explain it all."

Jason felt as if he had been hit with a hammer. *Good news? Oh God. How wonderful.*

Jefferson did not make him wait. He motioned for Jason to have a seat and began his report. "Jason, I do have good news for you. Your uncle Tomas has had a hearing and will soon be where he will create no more trouble. My detective did some good work and soon had the pawnbroker confessing to helping Tomas set you up as being a thief. When he confessed, Tomas's attorney did as well. So we had two confessions, and your uncle finally admitted his guilt. You have been exonerated, and your inheritance was placed in a bank here in Seattle. The Vermont attorney's assistant, John Confers, will join us shortly. He will fill you in on all the details, including a bill for his charges and those of the detective I hired. I have a new application for you to fill out. It will ensure your admittance to Washington State College. But I have already placed your name on the list of incoming students."

They beamed at each other for a few minutes, Jefferson feeling elated and contented. Jason was on a cloud in a euphoric daze. Relief washed over him as he realized that he had wished for a miracle, and here it was.

"How can I ever thank you for all you have done? You have made a miracle happen, and I will be ever grateful."

"I only did what I thought right. I am happy to have been able to help you and Lyndell." Jason shook his hand again and, with a light heart, started home to tell the good news.

When he arrived back at the Mission House, he found lots of busy hands. They were going to celebrate Jason's "miracle." Rosa had put three chickens in the oven to roast, along with some large potatoes. Several others had chopped salad greens and tomatoes. A bottle of wine had appeared as if by magic, and several loaves of French bread graced the table. There were flowers in vases and a plate of cookies waiting for dessert. Were those several milk bones alongside the cookies? Yes, they had not forgotten Duke.

Jason was touched by all their kindness. He hadn't thought they knew that much about his problems, but here they were about to celebrate his happy news. They ate, drank the wine, sang some songs, and wished him and Lyndell happiness. "Here's to a good life." A little tipsy, they all decided to wait until the morning to clean up.

Jason followed Lyndell upstairs to their room. Still feeling the effects of the wine, he sat and watched Lyndell get ready for bed. She seemed unaware of him sitting by the window, his eyes following her every move. He was aware of how hard he was and shifted in his chair to ease his discomfort. Didn't she know he was aware of her? Was this an invitation to get closer?

When she finally drew back the covers and lay down, he went into the bathroom and showered. When he came back, she was still awake and looking at him with those expressive large eyes. He pulled back the covers and lay down next to her. His arm pulled her closer, and she sighed and moved closer to him. He needed no more encouragement, and soon, he was kissing her and whispering loving words.

Jason's hands were tender as he caressed her body, first her back and sides and then her breasts. "Oh God, Jason." She was trembling with a need she had never known. A warm deep throbbing gave way to a yearning for more. She moaned and moved her hips in invitation.

Can I believe it? Does she really want me too?

"Lyndell, if we don't stop now, I won't be able to. If you don't want this, now is the time to say so."

Like being hit with a dash of ice water, she shivered and backed away. "I guess I got carried away—what with the wine and all. We had best stay good friends. Jason, I'm sorry I wasn't thinking straight."

"It's all right, Lyndell, but from now on, we sleep in different rooms. I can't take any more of these mixed signals."

Lyndell went quite still. She felt stiff and almost unable to breathe. "Yes, I know this is not fair to you. My past is ever in the way."

Bristling with anger, he said, "Well, damn it, do something about it. If we talk it over, it may turn out to be just another bump in the road. Do you think I'd hold something in your past against you? Do you want to let a dark event from your teens mar your whole life? Think about it. When you are ready to share it with me—ready to trust me—let me know. I love you, Lyndell, but I won't be put on 'hold' forever."

Anger in his every movement, he turned away. He lay as quiet as he could and tried to shut out his disappointment and frustration. His breathing was ragged as he tried to calm his frustration. *What a crappy ending to such a wonderful day.* Sleep was a long time coming.

Tears ran down Lyndell's face. She thought about all that had been said. His pride had been hurt too much this time to ever try again. Was she being a fool? Could he possibly want her if he knew about Gabby? Exhausted, she finally slept—a restless sleep, full of menacing shapes and dark shadows.

In the morning, Jason felt a bit ashamed. He had tried to take advantage of Lyndell's reaction to the wine. He knew she wanted him. She was holding fast to her past hurts. For some reason, she thought he would not listen in love or be nonjudgmental. Whatever it was, it had to be brought to light. Only then could they have a future together.

When Lyndell opened her eyes, Jason was sitting on her side of the bed. He smiled a sort of lopsided grin. "Good

morning, sleepyhead. It's time we did the breakfast routine.
Let's put last night away for now. It's a new day and time for
some changes.

"Yes, changes. Now that we have money in our account,
we can look for an apartment. I'd like it to be close to the
college. I'd like to be able to walk to the college, if possible.
Perhaps a high school will be close as well."

"Today? Rosa will be happy at that. If we can move today,
she can give the room to another needy person. She has been
very patient with us. We've stayed here for what—eight
weeks now?"

"Yes, we have. When we leave here, I want to give her
a donation for the Mission House. I haven't forgotten the
money I owe you either. I'll figure it out and have it ready for
you in a day or two. Thanks again for being my best friend.
When I needed one, you were there." He leaned over and
kissed her—a gentle kiss with a promise.

CHAPTER ELEVEN

They found that apartments close to the college were not very promising. They were very expensive and would allow no pets. They each read and reread the paper's offerings. Nothing was available that they could afford. "Well," Jason said, "we're close to the Wayside Chapel, so why don't we stop and say hello to Reverend Johnson? He'll be happy to hear our good news."

Lyndell nodded and thought it would be nice to give him a gift. "Why don't we give him some herbal tea?" Lyndell said. "Sounds good to me," replied Jason. They turned and retraced their steps to a store that sold specialty food.

When they arrived at the chapel, they found Reverend Johnson working on his Sunday sermon. He welcomed them with a smile, as he was really stuck for ideas. "Come in, come in," he greeted them. "I need a break for sure."

"I'm sorry we have not been to see you as often as we'd like. We have been trying to catch up on chores we do at the Mission House, and today we are apartment hunting. Reverend Johnson, we have some really good news to tell you."

Jason told him of his good fortune and said it was a miracle. "Mr. Wilder was able to hire a detective and an attorney in Vermont. They found my story to be true and were able to prove it. My uncle will be behind bars for a good while. I have my name cleared and my inheritance restored. I can now afford to go to college and study what I want."

Reverend Johnson beamed. "Let's give a prayer of thanks. Miracles, it seems, do happen." Lyndell and Jason bowed their heads, and as Reverend Johnson spoke, his words brought peace to each of them.

"So tell me, Jason, how is the apartment hunting going? Have you found anything you like?"

"Not at all good, I'm afraid. There are few available and all too expensive. Besides, they don't allow dogs."

"Don't be discouraged. Let me think for a moment.

"You know, my neighbor Charlie Lieu has a small cottage behind his house. He used to rent it for the summer, but this year, he had some major repairs to do, and it has been empty while the work was done. The repairs are all finished, and he may be willing to rent it to you—especially since it would be for a few years. He'd like that."

"It sounds great, but how about Duke? He's a part of us now. We love him and have to have him with us."

"Let me call Charlie and see what he thinks. He knows me and will accept my recommendations for you and Duke."

Charlie was delighted with the offer to rent the cottage for the years Jason would be going to college. He loved dogs, and it was fine to have Duke, as long as he was not destructive.

Lyndell and Jason sat in shock. Their worries about housing were over? Just like that? This was another miracle to add to the many since coming to Seattle. Jason was so happy he said the unexpected. "Shall we say another prayer, Reverend Johnson?"

Pleased with the request, Reverend Johnson was quick to bow his head and comply.

A few days later, Lloyd called and offered to take them to see the cottage and meet Charlie Lieu. "I can take you tomorrow morning, and Charlie will be home then. He is a very nice person and teaches at Washington State."

The next morning, they were off to see the cottage, braving a downpour. Duke came with then, and the car was soon damp with Duke's shaking off the rain. "We should have brought a towel," said Lyndell.

"Yes," replied Jason. "I'm sorry I didn't think of it."

Lloyd said, "When we get to Charlie's, we can borrow one and quick dry everything. It is only water."

Lyndell smiled at Lloyd. She was unused to people being so nice. Her stepfather would have hit the dog and her too, if it had been his car. *I'll never get used to people being this kind.*

It didn't take long for an agreement to be reached between Charlie and Jason. He had petted Duke and had no trouble accepting him. Jason would pay a very fair rent and would also cut the grass and tend the flower beds as part of the deal. They shook hands, and Charlie said they could move in one week from today.

When Rosa heard a knock on the door, she thought it might be the two lovers returning. However, the burly man and his companion wore ugly faces and tried to push the door open.

She called for Jose, a young man staying there, to come quickly. He did and gently pushed Rosa aside in order to confront the strangers.

"I am Stanly Nickerson, Lyndell's stepfather. Lyndell is legally my stepdaughter, and I want her right now, lady. I have come a long way to find her. She is lawfully my charge. She ran away from her home and is in violation of the law. She is going back with me."

Rosa said, her voice hard as steel, "You had better leave or I will call 911. Lyndell is with her husband, and I have never heard of you."

Jose made his fists obvious and shoved the men back out the door. "If you come back, you had better bring the police with you. Get off the property and stay off. Is that clear?" He slammed the door and gave Rosa a hug. "That's not the end of them, I guess. Somehow I feel they mean trouble. Lyndell and Jason will be upset." He shook his head as he went back to the kitchen.

As soon as she could, Rosa called Reverend Johnson. She was so excited she could hardly be understood. Finally, he got the message and said, "Rosa, Jason and Lyndell are at Charlie Lieu's house. I will call them and let them know what has happened."

When Jason and Lyndell were told of her stepfather's visit, Lyndell panicked. Trembling, she sat and rocked back and forth. "Oh no, oh no," she moaned over and over. Jason sat and thought about what they could do.

He filled Charlie Lieu in on what had been going on in Lyndell's life and then said, "We should marry right away. Then he can't touch her."

When Charlie had understood everything, he agreed. "Reverend Johnson could marry you in a few days. Then you and Lyndell could move into your house, even if it is sooner than we planned. If they come here, I will personally boot them away. And Duke will be ready for them as well."

Lyndell sat, as in a trance, as information about getting a marriage license was researched. Yes, they could get a license today, Thursday, and could be married Monday. A blood test was not required, so there should be no problem. They were going to be driven to the courthouse by Lloyd and obtain the necessary document. Before she knew it, she was in the car heading to the courthouse.

"Wait, Jason. This is not a good idea. You're moving too fast. You don't know everything about me. I have things in my past that may not be acceptable to you. I just can't tell you right now."

Jason did not answer for a moment. "Lyndell, you have one option. Go back with your stepfather, Stanly, and Gabby, or marry me. Which do you want?"

She sat in silence for a few minutes. "I guess marriage is the answer, Jason, but you may not love me enough to forgive my past."

He took her in his arms and kissed her. "Does that answer your fears and doubts? I love you, Lyndell, and I know you love me, and that's all that matters."

CHAPTER TWELVE

Rosa's face was beaming as she watched Jason and Lyndell climb the steps to the Mission House. "What great news! Reverend Johnson just called to tell me of your wedding plans. I hope you will let me help you all I can. You can have a reception here. We will all be happy to share your joy."

Lyndell, still in a daze, nodded her head. She slowly walked to the stairs and wearily climbed up to her room. Her bed beckoned, and she almost fell into it. Within a few minutes, her eyes were closed in sleep.

When she awoke, the sun had almost set. Lying quietly, she let the soft twilight soothe her troubled mind. *I have one other option. If I hurry, I can leave. A bus would soon take me away from having to face the past. It would also take me away from the only person who has ever loved me aside from my mom. Mom was so loving—so warm. Well, if Jason and I are to ever have a happy life together, I have to tell him everything.*

The door opened, and she could tell by the look on Jason's face that she had run out of options. She had waited too long. But Jason just held out his arms, and she went into them with a sigh of relief. He held her for a while. He didn't say anything, just held her.

Dinner was a happy affair for everyone but Lyndell. She gave it her best effort, but she was too worried to relax. Jason understood, and after they had cleaned up the dining room and kitchen, he asked if she would like to take a walk.

Glad for the exercise, she got Duke's lead, and they were ready to leave. But as they were going out the front door, they saw a car draw up to the curb. Without a sound, they hurried back into the house and locked the door.

They told Rosa what they had seen and asked her not to open the door but stay inside with the door locked. They quietly opened the back door and slipped outside. They quickly walked into the wooded area behind the house. The path there would take them to the park a few blocks away.

Jason said, "I think it best to elude them until we are married. Then they can't cause us any trouble and will have to leave."

She gave him a grateful look, as she didn't need any more hassles with her stepfather. In a few days, they would be free, and Jason could hire an attorney to help her regain her trust fund.

They watched Duke as he raced around the area. Then they started down the walking path, Duke leading the way. When they came to some picnic tables, they sat, and Jason looked at Lyndell, his eyes full of love.

"Lyndell, we have a private moment here. Why don't you tell me what is so terrifying that you are afraid to trust me? We are to be married in a few days, so tell me, I am not going to be judgmental."

She nodded. Yes, it was time for confessions.

"Jason, my mother died when I was very little—not quite twelve years old. My stepfather was decent until then. But after she died, he began to drink. He hoped to drown his sorrows, but it just made him mean. He became a tyrant. I had to come straight home from school and do chores. I had no friends, nor was I able to play sports. I had to learn to cook and clean up, and then if I wasn't too tired, I could do homework. I managed to keep up my grades, but just barely.

"Then when I was sixteen, he met Gabby. They became fast drinking buddies, and things got worse after that. Gabby used to try to pull me into his lap and fondle me—touch me where he shouldn't. They thought it was funny, but I was scared. I told my stepfather if Gabby touched me again, I would go to my teachers and the police and tell what Gabby was doing.

"Gabby left me alone then, but still, I felt fear when he looked at me with his penetrating glittering eyes. When he came to visit my stepfather, I hid in my room and locked the door.

"One day, I was too sick to go to school. I had a vicious headache, and my tummy hurt with sharp pains. I felt a little dizzy and feverish. It was about three o'clock when I heard the footsteps. They were heavy coming up the stairs. I shook with terror as I knew who it was.

"When he opened the door, he gave a weird chuckle. 'Oh, you're in bed waiting for me. Now I'm going to get my revenge, girl. I have been dreaming of this and how this moment would be.'

"He came to the bed and pulled the covers back. He stood and looked at me, his face an evil mask. I tried to scream, but he slapped me. Then he ripped my gown until it was shreds.

He removed his shoes, socks, pants, and underwear. All the time I kept moaning, 'Don't do this, Gabby. Please don't do this. I am so sick. Please …'

"He got in bed and straddled me. He pawed at my breasts and then began to push inside me. A rush of pain made me gasp, and all at once, like a geyser erupting, I vomited. Oh God. Again and again, I spewed all over us. The stench was so vile Gabby swore and pulled away. He gave me one hard slap and said, 'You little bitch. I'll get you for this. Gabby never forgets or forgives.'

"I must have passed out, for it was late afternoon when I came to. I felt so filthy, so defiled. I got up and removed the soiled sheets. I then went into the bathroom and took a long hot shower. When I cleaned up my room and put the bedding into the washer, I crawled back into the cleanly made bed.

"At dinner that night, I told my stepfather that I had been sick all day and couldn't make dinner. He grumbled but sent for a pizza … just one, for him.

"It was the next morning that I overheard my stepfather and Gabby talking. They were in the kitchen having coffee, and my door was open. Clearly, I heard my stepfather say, 'If I can get Lyndell to marry you, we could have control of the trust fund that her mother left her. It's about $60,000 or more. She gets it when she is twenty-one or on the day she marries if it is before that. She's so scared of me that she just might do it. If not, I'll think of another way. I did have a plan, but it wouldn't work. However, I've beaten her into being agreeable several times in the past.'

"It was a Saturday, so I had no school. I heard them go out and quickly packed a duffle bag with clothes and food that would keep. I put in a flashlight and then some money from the pouch that held my stepfather's booze money. The pouch was hidden in his bathroom, but I had seen him go there and get money once or twice. I counted out twenty dollars and put the rest back. I dressed extra warmly and put on my heaviest boots. I ran out the back door and headed toward the lake. I hoped there would be a summer cottage that I could get into for a while.

"That's when I found you, Jason. I wish I did not feel so soiled, but I still do. I think you deserve someone who has no hang-ups or troubling past."

"Oh, Lyndell, you are so wrong. I love you just as you are. Your past is not your fault. You are a victim of your stepfather's cruelty. You are beautiful inside and out. I will be happy to have you as my partner and lover for the rest of my life."

Jason put his arms around her, and his kiss was so tender, it left her shaking with desire. A door had closed, Lyndell thought. But a new one had opened. It was a door to happiness, a door to a new life.

CHAPTER THIRTEEN

Rosa looked out of the living room window. She saw a car parked at the end of the driveway. Inside the car, she could see two men. They looked like the ones who were here the other day and were so ugly. Oh no! They had a shotgun. Were they going to shoot Duke? She clutched her throat to keep from crying out. She ran into the kitchen and got out her special book. In it were the phone numbers of the local police station. A familiar voice answered after two rings.

"Hello, Mike, this is Rosa from the Mission House. I am afraid I may be wrong, but I had to let you know."

"Let me know what, Rosa? Calm down and speak slowly. I am here to help you."

"Well," Rosa began. As quickly as she could, she explained, "There are two men in a car just outside in our driveway. They were here before and were ugly and threatening. One man said he is Lyndell's legal stepfather and the other a fiancé they want to take Lyndell back to Vermont. I believe they have a gun and plan to shoot Duke. They were chased away by Duke the last time they were here. I told them to leave or I'd call 911.

They left, but I had the feeling they meant harm to Lyndell. Now they are in a car parked at the driveway entrance, and I saw a shotgun in the car, pointed at the house."

"I will be there in a blink, Rosa, with backup. Lock the doors, keep out of sight, and don't open the doors to anyone." Rosa nodded, as if he could see her. She only had a short wait before two squad cars pulled into place, one in front and one in the back of the parked car.

Mike looked the two men over and decided they were two of the meanest-looking guys he'd seen in a while. "Your license?" he asked curtly. "I also want to see your permit for the gun."

Stanly sputtered but gave the gun to Mike. Mike gave it to his deputy, Jerry, to check the serial numbers. "Did you buy the gun here?" Mike asked.

Stanly shook his head. "No, I bought it in Vermont."

"How did you bring it here? Did you drive here? Did you come by train or by air?"

Stanly mumbled, "By United Airlines."

"How interesting," Mike said. "They have such security now that you couldn't possibly bring a shotgun by any airline."

"You're right, Mike, it was stolen from a truck at the mall yesterday. The numbers match," Jerry said.

"So far we have two strikes against you, a stolen gun and harassment. Now, why don't you tell me what you two are doing here? Do you have business with the Mission House?"

Sputtering and suddenly afraid, Stanly said, "My stepdaughter has run away from home. She is only seventeen and under my care. I want her to come home. She has promised to marry this man, Gabby Pierce, her fiancé. I have a legal right to make her come home with me."

Mike looked at both men with disgust. "We are going to take you to the station, book you on stolen goods, and perhaps more. We will, of course, talk to your stepdaughter." Mike cuffed both men and drove off to the delight of Rosa, who had been watching.

When Jason and Lyndell returned, Rosa explained what had happened. Mike had requested their appearance at the station as soon as possible. "Don't worry," Rosa said, "I don't know what went on out there, but Mike put handcuffs on both men, and they drove away. Mike is a fair man and will listen to all sides. He's one of the best."

At the station, Lyndell was reassured that telling her story would be just for this once, and Mike would do everything possible to make sure that justice was done. "Don't be afraid to speak up. That is the only way we can help you, by knowing the whole story."

When she finished telling them about her life with her stepfather, Mike sat in silence for a few minutes. "Thank you, Lyndell. That took courage. We can now press charges, not only of theft and harassment but also of rape. However, that would involve time and public knowledge, and since there was a delay in reporting it, it's possible he could be cleared of rape. However, there's another solution. We would not press the rape charge but would keep the charges of a stolen gun and harassment on record. Your stepfather must return all of your trust fund immediately. There will be a fine levied for the stolen gun charge. They then may both leave Seattle, but with the threat that retuning here could mean a trial and prison.

"This way, there would be no media coverage, and you would be free to live here in peace. Think it over, and we can talk again in a little while."

Jason and Lyndell went to a nearby café for some tea and Danish. "Jason, what do you think I should do? I know I did not report the rape right then, and it would be hard to convict him on that. I feel so unsure. I need to have closure on this. If I don't press charges, I want to be certain that I receive my inheritance. My mom left me quite a lot of money, and I don't want him to get it."

"Lyndell, the decision is yours. I agree that if we can avoid a trial, it would be in your best interest. I think Mike can make sure Stanly does not get any of your money, as a result of your amnesty. It may take a few weeks, but you should have any money that is in your trust fund."

After a thoughtful moment, Lyndell nodded. They returned to the courthouse and told Mike what she had decided. He nodded and said it was probably the best way to resolve it. "There will be a return of the money in your trust fund before the men will be released. Also, a fine of $1,000 is going to be charged for stealing the gun and is to be paid before we close the case—for now. The threat of a future reopening of the charges, if they ever return, will be put in writing."

Jason and Lyndell were free to go after promising to be at the station to clear up any loose ends on Monday. Lyndell almost skipped out the door; she was so happy to have her ugly past behind her. "Oh, Jason, what a day this has been. I feel so lighthearted and happy."

Jason hugged her and whispered, "Let's celebrate at dinner tonight."

Tuesday was a day of soft rain and mist. It did not mar the joy of the wedding guests. The Wayside Chapel was decked in flowers and filled with music. Reverend Johnson wore his vestments with pride as he prepared to help Jason and Lyndell speak their vows.

Jason looked at Lyndell, as she moved slowly toward him. His heart almost stopped. She was so beautiful. Her face was radiant, and her eyes were glowing with love. Her dress had been made for her by Rosa and some of the women at the house. It was cream colored, trimmed with pale pink lace. Her bouquet of pink roses completed the picture.

Lyndell thought Jason was the most handsome man she had ever met. He wore a dark blue suit that fitted his muscular frame to perfection. His shirt was white and his tie several shades of blue. His eyes met hers, and she saw a promise—his promise of tender and lasting love.

With lots of fanfare, they all arrived back at the Mission House for the reception. Rosa had prepared a simple but delicious lunch complete with a two-tiered wedding cake. Duke was not forgotten and on a special plate were two varieties of dog treats.

When the festivities were over at the Mission House, Jason and Lyndell went to their new home. Jason said, "Let's have a second celebration." They found champagne and a snack for them, a gift from Rosa. Another surprise was for Duke. There was a soft and roomy dog bed—placed just outside their bedroom door. Duke sighed and circled before claiming it. Who thought he wanted a fancy bed? Again, he sighed and then closed his eyes. It had been a big day.

CHAPTER FOURTEEN

Lyndell's nightgown was made of fine cotton. It felt so soft against her skin. It was trimmed with satin roses. She had brushed her hair until it shone. One wedding gift had been of a flowerlike fragrance. She wanted to be perfect for Jason.

Jason turned back the covers and invited Lyndell to join him. On a table close to the bed was the chilled bottle of champagne. Some brie and crackers were arranged neatly on a plate. Rosa had thought of everything, Jason thought. He turned to Lyndell and said, "Lyndell, I am going to do some magic, and I want you to take off the lovely gown." *Did he say magic? What's he up to? He has that look in his eyes that means mischief.*

Without a word, Lyndell took off her nightgown and lay down on the bed. Jason kissed her. It was a tender kiss, full of promise. "Over on your tummy, sweetheart." She rolled over, but her heart was racing. *What was he up to?*

He poured a little creamy lotion on his hands. He straddled her and began a gentle massage. From her neck to her toes, he paid homage to her lovely body. Lyndell felt warm and tingly. She wanted more, but she didn't know just what. Jason helped turn her over, and again, his hands treated her to a loving, gentle touch. "Lyndell, I want to erase every touch of HIS hands. I want you to be free of the memory. It is over; my hands will take his evil touch away. I am giving you love through my hands to heal you. Can you feel it, sweetheart? Can you feel the love I have for you?"

She couldn't speak but sighed in dreamy pleasure. When he finished, she lay in a daze. Her body felt tingly and needing more. He then did something to her so incredible, she gasped. He rained kisses from her neck to her toes. Then he began an assault with his tongue, leaving her crying his name and begging for release. Again and again, he kissed her and fondled her. His fingers found her nest of soft downy hair. He gently rubbed her until she moaned with need. Jason kept on kissing her and fondling her until she was making pleading sounds that she wasn't aware of. He felt she was ready for him, and he positioned himself and slowly pushed inside. She gave a sharp cry, and he almost withdrew. *Was she a virgin? Perhaps Gabby had not gotten his revenge.*

Knowing he had hurt her, he tried to stop. However, he couldn't. Gently, he began the mating dance, an age-old sweet melding of two people in love.

"Lyndell, my darling," he urged, "go with me now—to the stars and back. Do you feel my love? Do you know that I adore you?"

The climax came with Lyndell crying out Jason's name. There was a moment of intense delight before they drifted down to earth again. They fell asleep, still embracing and at peace.

CHAPTER FIFTEEN

The leaves were turning color slowly. The days had passed quickly, and summer's end had found Jason and Lyndell busy with their new home. Lyndell had planted some fall flowers, and the grass was cut to perfection. Jason had been getting ready for college to begin, and Lyndell had been attending high school at night to earn her GED.

Duke was happy in their new home. He had room to run and was a constant joy to both Jason and Lyndell. He slept in his comfy bed but missed sleeping with Jason and Lyndell.

Last night, Duke had been restless. He lay in his bed outside of their door with his eyes wide open. He thought he had heard something. Duke lifted his head. All was quiet. There was no sound. Again, he listened. Yes, there it was again. He cocked his head, and his eyes gleamed for a moment. Then he rested his head on his paws and drifted off to sleep.

It was rainy the next day. The soft rain beat down on the windows. Jason sat at the kitchen table reading over the mail he'd received earlier. His concentration was rapt as he absorbed all the data. "Lyn, come look at this. The required courses are outlined in blue and the others in green. I know I'm going to enjoy all this.

"The first one is an overall view or an introduction to oceanography. It is course 101. Then there are more, each one adding new areas for study. They cover the ocean floor, underwater volcanoes, and even evolution. There are also courses on depth of the various oceans, fish of all types, and their food. Then, when I have passed all my required courses and am ready, there is a course of five to six weeks aboard a submersible vehicle. I'll get to look at everything firsthand and not from a book."

Lyndell felt his excitement. He was so keen and had overcome much to be here. "Jason, I am so proud of you. I know you will do well with your studies and your work."

"Thanks, Lyn. How about you? You are almost ready for graduation yourself. I am so proud of you."

"Well, it is only a GED. But yes, I am happy that I am almost ready for the next step in our plan."

"Then it's community college for you, right?"

"Yes, I have already looked over the offerings at the one near here. I think I want to become a paralegal. It sounds like interesting work, and I'll get to learn a lot about laws and legal procedures."

Jason got up and hugged her. "That sounds like an interesting choice, Lyn. I know you'll do well." He looked around the room. "Where's Duke? He's not in the house, is he?"

"Oh, he was pacing, and I thought he might want to be outside, now that the rain has finally stopped."

"Did you ever wonder, Lyn, how he came to find you? It is as if he knew that you needed a friend, someone to be your guardian angel."

"Yes, I have often thought of that. It almost seems as if he had been sent to me." She sighed. "We'll never know, will we?"

"No, we were the lucky ones to have him find us. He has been our guide since that first day. Come on, Lyn. Let's let him go for a run while we watch the rainbow." They went outdoors and looked up at the sky. The rainbow was impressive. Its colors were brilliant as it arched over the land.

"Isn't it amazing to see that promise of joy and beauty to come?" Jason asked. "It reminds me of the hopes and promises of life. Of course, we have to do our part too. I always love to see it there above us, never changing but pointing the way."

Jason's arm around Lyndell made her feel secure. Love and a beckoning future, she thought, were gifts at the rainbow's end.

They opened the gate for Duke to have more space to run, but he just stood outside of the gate and sniffed the air. He cocked his head and gave a soft woof ... He looked at Jason and Lyndell with his brown eyes filled with love. He gave another woof and began walking toward the road.

"Oh, Duke, come back. Don't leave us."

Jason put his arms around her and gave her a kiss on her cheek. "I think he has to leave us, as he has heard a call. Someone needs him, just like we did. I believe he will not forget us but will come back when he can."

Duke looked over his shoulder one last time but then turned and kept a steady trot toward the main road. It seemed as if he was following the rainbow as it arched out and beyond.

The mist almost hid him, but he turned one more time. He looked at them for a long moment and then turned and disappeared near the rainbow's end.

"He's gone," Lyndell sobbed. "He's really gone."

Jason held her and stroked her back to soothe her. "Yes, Lyn, I think he heard a call ... Perhaps there's someone who needs him more than we do."

"Thank you, Duke," Lyndell said. "We will always remember you. Take our love with you wherever you go."

Jason kissed her and held her tight as they stood and watched the rainbow until it faded from view.